THE
BEAST
OF
MOSCOW

A SAGA

BETHANY-KRIS

PART ONE

For every woman who loves a beast.

CONTENTS

1.

"*Putain*—mighty scar, that."

Vaslav only arched a brow at the comment from the Frenchman sitting across from him in the black SUV. He much preferred to drive himself, and often used to when he spent most of his year in Moscow, but business always called for a driver. Not to mention, the privacy afforded by the blacked-out windows of the Mercedes limo.

"A knife?" the man asked. "Looks like a knife scar to me."

A sigh answered that question.

He could have had this quick meeting without the conversation but considering his driver had not yet found a suitable place to park, Monsieur Pierre Aubert proved himself to be one of *those* people. The type that needed to fill the silence with anything just because.

Vaslav *hated* those kinds of people.

At the same time, he peered out the darkly tinted

windows, the SUV pulled off the road and rocked roughly as the limo slipped down a dirt path that ended at the edge of the Moscow Canal. He rarely came this close to Dubna during the week if he was doing business. Otherwise, he preferred to hide away behind the walls of his private estate as much as his duty would allow.

"Are we—"

"A razor blade, no?" Vaslav said, drawing the attention of the Frenchman to him instead of the way the limo parked alongside the canal. Already midday, one couldn't tell considering how dimly lit the rear of the limo remained. Just the way he liked it. "My bunkmate in detention thought I'd look better with a wider smile."

At that, Vaslav grinned.

He knew what it did to his face, and so did Pierre considering the color drained from the man's cheeks instantly. Stretching out the grisly scar on the right side of his mouth with a smile showed that despite the injury happening when he was sixteen in a juvenile colony meant to house him until he moved into an adult prison at eighteen—well, here he was thirty years later, and it was still as puckered, red, and angry as it had ever been. Jagged straight through his thick, neatly trimmed beard.

The fix had been shoddy. Two subsequent fights ripped the scar open again. Thankfully, he'd been able to fight off a later attempt by the leader of a rival gang to match up the uninjured side after a disagreement over territory lines in the prison yard.

Not that it mattered. Six months after the yard incident, shortly before his twenty-eighth birthday, he'd been freed.

Sort of.

If a man wanted to call his kind of life *freedom*.

At least, the scar didn't hurt anymore. One of the only things that no longer caused Vaslav pain. Everything else was still up in the air.

"What do you think, comrade? I was told it gives me a little … *something. Da?*"

The Frenchman was quick to clear his throat and put on a friendly smile. If only it didn't twitch at the edges. "I-I'm sorry—*pardon me,* Mr. Pashkov. I don't mean to offend."

Vaslav let out a hard breath and gestured with one heavily tattooed hand, the inked rings on his fingers and upturned spider on his hand covered decades' worth of scars from fights, hard labor, and *life.* All the man across from him likely saw was the tattooed hand of a criminal, adorned with gold and glittering diamonds, cutting fast between them to signal his remaining, fleeting patience. "Curiosity killed more than just a cat—where is the coke?"

Right to the point.

He was all talked out, now.

Pierre slumped back into his seat, not bothering to hide his displeasure in the form of a scowl while he patted the pockets of his navy-blue suit blazer. As he pulled out a small, black balloon tied at the end, the man muttered, "*Dix mille à cet tête de noeud*—Christ. Here."

Arching one thick, dark brow high, Vaslav took the balloon of what should be pure, *prime* cocaine smuggled straight from the mountains of Italy where the production and trafficking of the drug were at an all-time high thanks to a mafia-like cartel based out of Palermo.

Not that he intended to visit—he only wanted a new supplier.

"Ten thousand, yeah, that's what you said?"

Pierre's gaze widened, lifting to meet the man's across from him, and he didn't hide the fear Vaslav found staring back. Maybe he couldn't. "I didn't realize you speak—"

"Do you know the kinds of people I have sat down with over the decades? *All kinds*," he told his counterpart, his expression never flickering from his calm, cold demeanor. "You pick up on the little things. Don't look too far into it."

God knew Vaslav had absorbed too much.

"What was the bet?" Vaslav asked.

Rolling his eyes as Vaslav produced a small, gold pocketknife from his pocket, the Frenchman admitted, "That you couldn't be as bad as they said; even a beast can laugh."

Well, he earned a chuff, at least.

For that.

Piercing the balloon with the tip of the small blade, Vaslav dropped Pierre's gaze but only to see the perfectly milled, white powder that came out on the blade. As fast as the cocaine was there, it disappeared on his tongue when he lifted the knife and licked the substance away.

Instantly, his tongue went numb. He rolled it around his gums to get the same effect in seconds. It was pure, but he figured …

"Someone went through the trouble of making sure it was extra fine for me," he noted.

"Well—"

"Tell Mario we will begin a conversation about importing his product for my distribution. I will want it coming in as close to Moscow as possible, hmm? No fucking around—he's to make the call to me before the end of the month. He should have heard by now, I'm all about the details, yes?"

Pierre dragged in a heavy breath and took the balloon back when Vaslav offered it between the leather seats. The cocaine disappeared into his pocket once more, only a bit of spilled powder remained on the carpeted floor. "They say you don't like working with Italians."

Vaslav's lips pursed into a fleeting grimace. "What good Russian does?"

"*Oui*," Pierre replied quickly, "I'm happy to make a split being the go-between. Everybody likes peace."

That time, Vaslav chuckled. The prick almost earned himself the laugh he'd bet he could win. Fortunately for the Frenchman, because when Vaslav laughed … horrible things almost always followed.

"No, everybody likes money," Vaslav eventually said, shrugging under the lightweight of his red silk dress shirt. "Peace is sometimes the necessary evil we resort to in order to get what we want."

Pierre didn't have a chance to respond before the passenger door on the left side of the limo was wrenched open without warning. Midday light spilled into the rear of the vehicle, illuminating a sliver of yellow color across the black carpet and the leather shoes of both men.

It seemed his counterpart hadn't heard the front passenger side door open or close, never mind the figure of a man rounding the vehicle.

"What in the hell—"

"Get out," Igor uttered, his shadow blocking the light as he came to stand in the open door. Despite being shorter than Vaslav by only two inches, the leader of the obshchak side of his bratva's organization was still an impressive sight standing at his full six-foot-six height. With shoulders as wide as a barrel, he easily filled the space leaning inside the vehicle, and one couldn't miss Igor when he came strolling down the street. Pierre stilled, clearly unsure what he should do. "Out, I said. The meeting is over. You can walk back."

Vaslav only smirked at the confused glance the Frenchman sent his way at the order.

"You can't be serious. We drove for twenty minutes! My driver was waiting—"

"Don't take it personally, Frenchman," Vaslav replied as the guy was yanked out of the limo without grace or fanfare. At least, he was smart enough not to fight back. Igor was not known for his patience, but he had one hell of a punch. Igor climbed into the seat Pierre had vacated, and reached over to grab hold of the door, ready to swing it closed. He waited before doing so, just long enough for his boss to tell the flustered, scowling man outside, "This is simply how I like to handle my business. Take any complaints straight to hell—or better yet, take them back to that prick paying you in Italy. See how he likes it."

Igor slammed the door shut, and the limo left Pierre standing in a cloud of hot dust on the dirt road along the canal. It took far too long for the air conditioning inside to catch up with the mugginess they'd allowed in for Vaslav's liking, so he rolled the sleeves of his dress shirt up to his elbows and unbuttoned the third button just below his throat to give him some room to breathe.

Mid-July in Russia was peak travel time for tourists

because it was also the hottest period of the year, and currently, the heatwave crawling through Moscow left Vaslav in a worse mood than normal.

"When's Nico—"

"Ask *him*," Vaslav uttered behind his clenched teeth while he pressed his fingertips into his eye sockets, willing the pressure there to release.

"I will," his head of security was fast to say, his Russian smooth and calm, already hearing that sharp edge in his boss's words that were ready to cut on the next syllable. "We can put off the rest of the day, if you want, yes? It's Thursday; take an early, long weekend, Vas."

Migraines were his enemy. Constant since childhood and worse into adulthood, caused from years of abuse, followed by fighting to survive within the prison gangs that had dominated his early life, and head injuries according to the doctors that offered him nothing more than pills for pain. It was like knives behind his eyeballs stabbing straight down through to the base of his skull.

They came without warning and sometimes lingered for days. Other times, they spread out, lasting only for a dozen or so minutes before disappearing altogether ... only to come right back again and again throughout the day. The migraines were an unspoken burden he carried, and any of his men who were lucky enough to sit in his presence—*ever*—could tell the state of his pain, and the danger of his mood, simply by the tone of his voice.

It was the pain that made him vicious.

The pain turned him *mean*.

"No, I have one more thing to handle before I do anything else today."

"I'm sure it can wait until Nico gets back from his trip," Igor started to say. "Let him handle that stupid fuck in the city. He's done it before."

Vaslav ignored his man's comment. Sure, he was only trying to help, and while Vaslav considered no one a friend because life had taught him those didn't exist, Igor and Nico were the closest things he had to it. If he felt anything akin to camaraderie or loyalty to another human, besides perhaps his still-living mother, it was his right- and left-hand men.

His spies.

But right then, he just wanted Igor to shut the fuck up. Otherwise, Vaslav would have to make him do it and neither of them wanted that.

Strangely, he could stand to listen to others speak when a migraine started to creep up on him. *Barely.* It was the sound of his own voice, however, that felt like knives to his eardrums.

"I said, I have one more goddamn thing to do," he uttered low, the gravely hiss of his words promising his companion wouldn't say another thing unless he wanted to bleed for it, too, "and I intend on doing it. This time, he owes me money."

Or so he had recently learned through stumbling upon paperwork that Nico would have otherwise preferred to keep hidden from his boss regarding Vaslav's former brother-in-law and the company he owned known as *The Swan House.* The infamous house of ballet in Krasnye had a two-hundred-year-old legacy attached to the deed, and names on its dossier of dancers that graced the world's stages had been associated with everyone and anyone with any sort of power and control.

Royalty. Political. *Criminal.*

A lot of money moved through those doors.

And the second Feliks Abramov had his eight-pointed stars tattooed on his shoulders, a portion of every dollar his beloved Swan House made, legally or otherwise, was no longer his. That was the deal he made with the devil who sat in the seat before Vaslav, and he didn't care for the details as to why.

Igor didn't glance away from the windows during the stretch of silence between the two men, but Vaslav still saw the way his gaze widened a bit at the news of an unknown debt between the organization and the remaining piece of Vaslav's past. Across from the irritated boss, Igor's reply was lower than a whisper.

"He was your family once, boss."

"Not anymore," Vaslav deadpanned.

His last murder assured that. Despite the attention and mess it had caused him, a half of a decade ago, to deliver his former father-in-law's decapitated head in a white box topped with a bright red ribbon to Feliks was the least of his regrets.

If anything, he thought it made his position in the city *very* clear.

They didn't call him The Beast of Moscow for nothing.

2.

In the Stars.

It had been an appropriate name for the ballet retelling of Romeo and Juliet, but the title also made a rising ballerina believe it was a show with a role meant for her. The story of the star-crossed lovers destined for a tragic end took a year from the start of rehearsals to production night. Vera took to the stage as Juliet on the night of her twentieth birthday. Six years later, staring into the torn flyer stuck to a light pole outside the front entrance to the main lobby of The Swan House with her image in full costume, makeup, hair, and pointe shoes promoting the event still managed to give her the same butterflies in her belly.

Only now, it didn't feel all that great. It didn't even matter that the years had taken its toll on the flyer, leaving the colors almost entirely faded, she could still see the image and how it once looked, too.

It was forever imprinted in her mind.

She couldn't remember when she had first fallen in love with ballet. As far as she was concerned, she'd always loved it. Maybe from the second she was born, like Juliet destined to die with her lover, Vera Avdonin had been meant for pointe shoes and satin ribbons. Either way, the day her father had taken Vera to her first class, she never imagined doing anything different.

"Your name is gonna be in stars someday," Demyan would tell her competition after competition when she was barely ten and other girls on her team teased her relentlessly over the slightest mistakes.

Even inventing them sometimes.

She hadn't known it back then, but their bullying came from a place of jealousy and driven by the adults around them who constantly made them feel like they were never going to be enough. The mean girls from the past didn't actually leave when Vera managed to land a spot as a ballerina for the coveted Swan House at only sixteen—she simply became more confident.

Convincing her father to let her leave the States for a city like Moscow had been the harder part. Compromise came in the form of private security, a man known for his penchant to protect dangerous men, until she was eighteen.

And only because she threatened to run away, otherwise.

Vera had only been a little dramatic.

The thing is, she would have done it.

Vera was determined to be the ballerina in the middle of the stage, the most beautiful, all spotlights on her, and an entire crowd at the edge of their seats, waiting with bated breath for her next step; so much so that for most of her life, she'd lived and breathed the art, sacrificed education, and having a childhood just to be the very best she could be *en pointe*. Every day, all day.

Until she was that ballerina.

She'd loved ballet that much.

Don't you still?

Vera didn't have an opportunity to ponder the question she asked herself.

"You're late!"

The first shout came in Russian, ripping her gaze away from the flyer she must have walked by a thousand or more times but had only noticed it remained that day.

She didn't even have time to ask *why today?*

Hanging out of the large, black marble doors adorned with golden swans for handles, Klara—one of the company's ballerinas that agreed to help Vera make dance classes available to underprivileged children for free three nights a week at The Swan House.

If anything, it gave Vera something to do.

Or maybe just a reason to stay.

After all, she hadn't danced on stage in years.

In English, Klara said, "I figured when you didn't pick up my call that something was up. I've got the kids doing their warmup stretches, but I have to get to my own—"

"No worries, thank you," Vera interjected, forcing herself to smile and hoping the younger ballerina didn't notice what had her lingering out on the sidewalk of the grand Swan House instead of being inside teaching her ballet class.

The flyer.

Her fading star …

Klara looked like she was considering heading back inside The Swan House but hesitated for a moment. No doubt, the practice she spoke of was all the way at the rear of the old stone cathedral and monastery. Once owned by the Russian orthodox church, no one really seemed to know how it became the property of a private family that converted it into a house of ballet complete with several studios and an entire theater that seated up to three-thousand people.

Vera thought someone knew; they simply didn't want everyone else to know, too.

Klara eyed Vera as she climbed the few marble steps up to the doors, waiting until she was at the top before asking, "*Ty v poryadke*—are you okay?"

"*Da*," she tried to assure her. "I was just up late talking to my ma back in New York and woke up *way* too late."

She didn't mention that she'd gotten drunk after she hung up with her stepmother, Claire. Or that a part of her desperately wanted to leave Russia and her shattered dreams behind she simply couldn't seem to pull the trigger on doing so.

"And you're late," Vera told Klara. "Madame Lidia is going to give you hell. *Go.*"

The eighteen-year-old didn't need to be told again, but she waited at the front doors just long enough to hold the heavy oak open until Vera slipped inside.

"And thanks again for the kids!" she called to the girl's retreating back.

Klara only waved a hand high before taking the grand staircase that curved along the west wall of the massive entrance to The Swan House. Black marble greeted guests that were lucky enough to come inside.

Floors, pillars, and even the stairs. The outside had been painted the color where it could be, and the stone wall surrounding the massive property included black wrought iron grating across the top. The rich tapestries and heavy silk and satin curtains that fell to the floor in luxurious piles around every window and entrance was all nostalgic for Vera.

She remembered the first time she saw it, The Swan House with its towering golden spires and massive stature looming amongst the backdrop of the city, and the way her heart had raced as she stepped inside. It was hard not to be amazed and in awe of this place, and what it had promised to her.

It became home.

Still was.

That's why she had yet to leave.

Partly, anyway.

Vera crossed the mostly quiet entrance, the only sound coming from the squeaks of her runners against the marble floor, murmurs from somewhere upstairs and young laughter traveling beyond the hallway beneath the massive staircase. She headed into the hallway with her small canvas duffle bag emblazoned with the logo of the ballet company tossed over her shoulder. At least in the warmer months, she didn't have to waste time bundling up, so all she really had to do was change shoes and toss off her light windbreaker. She already had on her staple black leotard and tights. Even the compress wrap that kept her left ankle steady while she danced only took a few seconds to put on.

If the kids had only started their stretches, then she had a few minutes to work with before someone started to complain about her tardiness. Not that she thought anyone would. Vera might not have danced professionally for The Swan House since that last showing of In the Stars, but the city still knew her name and loved her all the same.

That was the last thing Vera wanted to think about, so she forced those thoughts to the back of her mind as she entered the lower gallery of the newest studio built inside what had once been one of many storage sections for the company in the massive building. It never served her well to walk into a room full of kids who seemingly adored her with a heavy heart—she swore those kids could see it every single time.

They deserved better than that.

The parents—and guardians—of the class of students that she could see already lined up along the barres against the wall of mirrors through the gallery windows stopped their conversation as she breezed straight through with a wave. Their greetings chased her into the changing room connected to the gallery, but no one followed her inside.

Pink and black and gold duffel bags lined the benches inside the changing room, and Vera dropped hers with the kids'. It took her no time at all to change out her outdoor shoes and into her sneakers after she'd wrapped her ankle. The warmer months were easier because the cold always brought an ache to the old break.

Vera had just stood up and fixed the waistband of her tights when one of the girls from her class made herself known in the changing room by clearing her throat. Eleven-year-old Nelli shrugged and scuffed the toe of her shoe against the floor when she realized Vera had noticed her standing there.

"No tights?" she asked in Russian although most of

the kids and people who came in and out of The
Swan House were fluent in English, too. Otherwise,
they tended to pick up on it considering many of the
ballerinas that studied here came from all over the
world, and English was often the common
denominator for many.

"Or shoes," Nelli muttered.

"That's okay. I'll leave an extra set in here and you
can change fast. No problem."

At that statement, the blue-eyed, dark-haired girl
who had reminded her of herself the first time she
laid eyes on her beamed up at Vera. "I tried to remind
Mik but—"

"Mikhail has a lot going on, right? Is he taking
summer classes again?"

Nelli shrugged but nodded. "I miss him."

"I bet."

The girl's older brother had taken custody of the
girl after an unfortunate accident killed their parents
two years earlier. The boy was only twenty. He barely
made enough money to scrape by but didn't give
up—between his college classes and his sister, Vera
bet time was thin. She didn't hold it against him when
Nelli showed up missing something.

Anything could be fixed.

What was most important was that he got her there
in the first damn place. Three days a week for three
hours, Nelli and the other kids waiting for Vera in
that studio were safe and warm and every single one
of them were loved.

By her, anyway.

"All right," she told the girl, "I'll be out in a
second. Your clothes will be waiting right here."

"You're the best, Vera."

Those words, tossed over the girl's shoulder as she raced down the changing room's corridor, managed to make Vera smile. Even though it didn't last long.

Vera hadn't needed to remain tied to The Swan House after her final act on their stage left her with a shattered ankle, and a future without professional or competitive dance. In fact, her recovery—if only mentally—might have been easier had she put a decent bit of distance between herself and the company.

But even back then, she'd cared too much about the family she felt like she had made and the rest of the people within these walls. They must have cared a lot about her, too, considering the number of kids and dancers that made it a point to visit Vera every day of her recovery from the devastating injury. Each time, they asked when she was coming back.

Not *if* she would.

It wasn't like she had needed the money; Vera came to Russia with a trust fund that already made her life far beyond comfortable. The Swan House had been beneficial to her bank account, too, once she debuted on their stage—and Feliks, that prick, well he certainly hadn't offered to pay her a dime after everything had happened.

It wasn't about the money because there wasn't any.

Vera just couldn't leave this place.

Even though it ruined her.

She couldn't say goodbye.

A part of her wished she could understand the heavy sadness that left her with—a constant weight inside her chest that she couldn't explain—but what good would understanding any of it do for her?

All these years later, Vera was still here.

She figured … it must be where she wanted to be. If not, she certainly hoped it was where she should be.

*

"Let's wrap it up, call that a day," Vera told the class of thirty kids. Only a handful were boys with the larger majority being girls. Instantly, the second she told the group that the class was over, a chorus of voices chased her to the stereo where she turned it off and disconnected it from the Bluetooth on her phone.

"Aww, can we try that again?" asked Sonya, the oldest of the group at twelve. The scholarships offered by The Swan House looked fondly upon the kids who trained in their free program if the talent and effort was there. Spots were extremely limited, though, but Sonya was one of those kids she knew the instructors were watching. "That last set of steps—can I run through it again?"

"You did it perfectly," she told the girl.

"Yeah, but—"

"Vera, will you dance for us before we go?" piqued Nelli, her voice rising above the other kids who all wanted to be heard as parents started to come to the doorway of the studio, waving them back to leave.

The moment the girl voiced the idea, every other kid who didn't want to finish up with the class decided to add their agreement with Nelli's choice.

"I don't know," Vera said.

"Please?"

"I only have my sneakers."

"*So?*"

Nelli even put her hands on her hips when she added for the other kids, "You let me practice in sneakers."

"*Once*," she returned fast, laughing.

"Please, Vera?"

How could she say no to that?

She danced so infrequently—steady practice only led to pain, and likely, further reinjuring her ankle. Even teaching, she wore sneakers because she didn't have the support she needed in pointe shoes. Not even satin slippers with a grip on the bottom would do the job.

Vera tried everything, but the reality was that she danced for love, now. Only occasionally, never with much seriousness involved, and always because she wanted to.

Nothing else was possible.

"Is she going to dance?" Vera heard a parent ask from somewhere behind her shoulder.

"I think so," another kid called back.

Vera only sighed.

Especially when the kids asked again, "*Please, Vera?*"

Honestly—who would say no?

3.

The last thing a man in Moscow wanted to find in his office at dinner time hours was Vaslav Pashkov. A man like him should be anywhere else at this time of day—wining and dining a woman, maybe, or handling business to rake in another few hundred million to pad his many bank accounts.

A person certainly wouldn't want to find the Russian crime boss already sitting behind their desk the second they walked into the room, but that was exactly what greeted Feliks in his office at The Swan House. Except the man was too busy arguing with the female close at his back to notice the bigger threat waiting for him.

The woman—if she was even that, because Vaslav thought she couldn't be older than eighteen—was erratic, and her waving arms only added to the venom in her Russian that she spewed at the man.

"You promised me—you said it was mine!"

Her black leggings and backless leotard gave away

that she was a dancer, but the fact she still had her pointe shoes on made Vaslav think she was probably higher in the company. Especially if she had a direct line to Feliks who did nothing more for the ballet house than handle money and sign paperwork.

He certainly wasn't instructing the ballerinas, and when the company had been at its prime doing a show a week before traveling the world for another year showing the same ballet outside of Russia, Feliks had done nothing more than soak up adoration and praise while raking in millions in the meantime.

He was the face for the public—handsome, still young at only thirty-five, and connected to all the right people in all the wrong ways.

A mouthpiece, really.

Feliks had little to no power otherwise.

Oh, Vaslav was sure the *suka* believed he had a higher purpose where The Swan House was concerned, even agreeing to become a part of his father's criminal empire just to get his name on the deed.

But what good had it done?

According to the paperwork Vaslav found, that Nico told him it didn't matter to the grander scheme, The Swan House had been bleeding money for nearly six years. The prestige it once held had slowly been dimming for years. Yes, they still produced world class ballerinas, but a lot of good it did when they were only making money headhunting them for other companies.

The personal loan Vaslav's right-hand man offered to Feliks to save his precious house of ballet might not have technically been *his* money, but since he owned the soul of all vory within the confines of this godforsaken country ... anything they were owed was his.

Technicalities be damned.

Especially if it meant Vaslav could finally use it as a reason to get rid of the bastard. The last remaining Abramov tied to the dynasty that had built the empire Vaslav now ran—Feliks had known he was next on the man's list to die the second he'd opened a present in this very room to find his father's head waiting inside.

He'd always been a piss poor brigadier. Never should have made it past the *brodyagi* of his father's bratva because he was practically worthless as a criminal when he'd been born to nothing but a silver spoon and pampered for most of his life. Too spoiled and unwilling to make a bloody mess out of his hands, but goddamn, he'd wanted those stars on his shoulders all the same.

Mussor—literal garbage—he wasn't seen as anything more to the men across Russia and the factions of their brotherhood that extended beyond the country. Who would touch that? Not if a vor had any respect for the code, anyhow. It wasn't as if the brotherhood would miss the man or look for vengeance.

Vaslav had done well to keep this much of a distance between the two while he waited for the attention to boil over after his last move on Feliks' father. That was the entire reason he hadn't known there was so much money missing from this side of his business.

Feliks had been a dead man walking for a long time. The clock had finally stopped counting down, and now someone else would have to answer for the fact that it had gone on this long. Vaslav intended on handling that issue soon, too.

"*Nyet!*" Feliks spun on the shrieking girl with a furious punch of his pointed finger right in her face. It stopped her on the spot, his trembling digit only inches from her turned up nose. Shorter than the man by a few inches, she didn't appear at all scared of him.

It almost made Vaslav chuckle.

Who would be scared of Feliks? A bitch's bark was always worse than its bite.

"That is enough," Feliks hissed at the girl.

She opened her mouth, likely to argue back with the man, but Vaslav simply didn't have the patience to sit there and wait for someone to notice him any longer. As it was, he had already been there too long, and Igor would be returning with the car and driver at any moment. The second he did, Vaslav needed to leave, a call would be made, and the cleaner should come—that was his orders.

Then, this would all be over. He would never hear the name Abramov even whispered in his presence again.

Igor couldn't do his job if his boss didn't first do his, so Vaslav chose to interrupt the two.

Clapping slowly from where he sat behind Feliks' ornate, gaudy desk carved from a single piece of wood and painted a glossy black, Vaslav smirked as two pairs of eyes turned on him. Even a scowl could make his scarred face look like quite a sight waiting in the shadows of a room, so he only grinned more when the girl sucked in a gasp and stumbled a step back.

"Love the show, but where's my dinner?" he asked them.

"*Der'mo,*" Feliks cursed under his breath.

Vaslav's clapping came to a sudden stop when he said, "Yes, comrade, you're certainly in a lot of shit at the moment, aren't you?"

"Feliks, what's wrong, should I cal—"

He didn't offer the ballerina a chance to say anything further before he had shoved her out of the room, ignoring her protests and questions at the same time. Vaslav at least allowed the man to get the female out of firing range before he stood from the squeaky office chair that smelled like old leather and cheap cologne.

That smell had his migraine from earlier flaring all over again, but other than the squint of his eyes and hard set of his mouth—which didn't leave his expression all that different from his norm—one wouldn't know Vaslav was suddenly in blinding pain.

Literally.

For a few seconds, it took his vision away.

By the time Feliks had yanked closed the heavy oak doors leading into his office, Vaslav had already rounded the desk.

"I didn't know you were coming, Vas."

The nickname was enough to get the asshole killed right there on the spot—he could count the number of people on one hand that he allowed to shorten his name as if they were *friendly*. Feliks most certainly was not one of them.

"Oh, didn't you?" he asked back. "Apparently, Nico's been cleaning up after you for a while. I think you saw me coming for a long time, no?"

The words hissed through clenched teeth, but he knew they still made an impact.

Spinning around to face Vaslav, Feliks face drained of color when the taller, older man came to rest against the front of his desk. Hooking one ankle over the other, Vaslav tightened his grip on the edge of the desk's glossy top, squeezing it for all it was worth to hide the sudden shakiness in his hands.

The pain was sharper than ever. Light spots and black dots danced in his vision. The doctors liked to use a scale—a simple one to ten with the lower end being the least amount of pain and ten topping out at the very worst. Daily, while the migraines were just fading in and out, he maintained a steady seven on the scale.

Enough to still need meds. A Demerol could put a decent dent in his pain scale when caught at the right time, but by seven, it was enough to make him sick to his stomach.

Enough to make him *so angry*.

Right then, it was a pure ten.

And Vas could barely breathe.

It was the worst possible time for his migraine to come in fast and heavy. He blamed it on the past week—with Nico out of the country on a personal trip with his whore of the month, that left Vaslav and Igor to handle the city and any business within it on their own. Five, or two, years ago that might not have been such a problem.

Now, with the migraines becoming more frequent and severe, aided by his constant stress and high blood pressure, he could barely make it to the end of the week without finding himself huddled over a toilet, puking his guts out from the pain, and roaring for someone to find him *anything* to make it better.

He'd tried everything.

Even his own mother, who had lived in the same estate in Dubna—since before his initial incarceration at just thirteen years old for beating her rapist to death in the street—decided in the last year that she couldn't stay within the same walls as Vaslav anymore. He was too much; his pain was no longer his own when he allowed it to bleed into every person around him.

He didn't blame her.

He didn't even blame himself, now.

Vaslav was simply trying to get from one day to the next, but he wasn't entirely sure of the reason why. Who wanted to live like *this*—why wasn't he already dead? A better man would have pulled the trigger by now. He was sure of it.

Maybe that was the problem.

He was a coward.

"Are you okay?" Feliks asked.

Vaslav's jaws clicked from how hard he clenched his molars to swallow back the pain before he uttered, "Why wouldn't I be?"

That time, his words came out hoarse. He'd taken punches to the head that felt better than the exploding fireworks of agony that rippled through his brain like the aftershocks of a wave.

He didn't meet the man's eyes. Couldn't reach for the gun to shoot the bastard like he had initially come there to do. Vaslav was only able to suck cool air through his tight teeth and then talk. The damn migraines had been fading in and out for a good day, but he knew what it meant because every time they came back in again, they were longer. Soon, he would get no break between the flashes of pain, and it would all melt together for a migraine that would last …

His longest had been nine days.

Of unending pain.

Igor was right.

He needed to take that early weekend and hide away behind the stone walls of his estate with the shades drawn tight on every window and a bottle of good vodka close. At least then when he started to puke, he couldn't blame it just on the migraines.

"Where is my fucking money?" Vaslav demanded.

He did meet Feliks' stare, then, only to find the younger man's cheek twitched with the lie he was about to spew. No surprise.

"You already know I don't have it or you wouldn't be here otherwise."

Hell.

Maybe the man wasn't a total fucking moron.

"This place has been—"

"It's not been the same since the accident," Feliks rushed to say.

Excuses, Vaslav knew.

Still, he let the man talk because it gave him a second to steady himself again. Maybe he could push down the pain long enough to get this over with.

"We couldn't sell a fucking ticket—every vendor in Europe canceled for the tour. There was too many problems, they said. *Rumors*. It practically ruined us."

Licking at his dry lips, Vaslav then asked, "Do you really think it matters now?"

He knew of the incident the man spoke of—an injured ballerina, a favorite of the company and public. Vaguely, the details stuck out in his mind but little else because that time in his life had been a particularly hard one. Those years followed the death of his wife and almost everything surrounding finding her murdered on the front steps of his estate, a shotgun blast through her face to ensure there would be no open viewing of her body before they buried her, well … he'd lived his days in a bit of haze.

Until one day, it all cleared.

And everybody paid.

Everybody.

And none of that changed what Vaslav intended to happen here today.

"Vas, you've gone white," he heard Feliks say. "You don't look okay."

When had the room swayed like that? Why was it so goddamn *bright?* One of his hands went numb, but the bigger issue was that he couldn't tell which.

Well, the ringing in his ears had finally started. Of that, he was sure. The second he let go of the desk, both his knees buckled. He was barely able to keep his formidable frame from crumpling to a heap on the floor.

A floor that was spinning beneath him.

Something was definitely wrong.

It was more than just the pain.

"Get Igor," Vaslav ordered, unable to watch Feliks' retreat from the room, but he thought he heard the footsteps receding. It was a toss-up whether the man even heard him call out, "He should be at the front."

By now.

Fortunately for Feliks, the rest of Vaslav's plan would have to wait.

4.

"Vas, are you even listening to me?"

"Don't you fucking *dare*," he heard himself snarl.

Had he pushed Igor off? He must have because from somewhere behind him, his steps stumbling one after another to propel him toward a set of large doors, his head of security shouted, "You can't barely stand—I'm calling one! Kill me later for it."

"*Otva'li*," Vaslav barked, but he thought it came out a little too garbled. The curse didn't have his sharp impact coming out of his mouth like it usually did.

Or maybe that was just the rest of the sounds around him that felt like they were all swirling together. He didn't recognize the hall he entered, but he was sure a different voice had added something into the conversation he left behind.

Something that sounded a lot like, "He can't go far. Call for help. I know he hates me, but goddammit, she'd never forgive me."

Vaslav wasn't sure what part of this he disliked the

most—that he couldn't remember where he was or the reason for why he was there. In fact, when he reached into his memories, he found a bank of still images, faces and moments that he understood and recognized without any uncertainty, but he couldn't remember where he had woken up that morning.

Still stumbling down the unfamiliar corridor, the argument continued to ensue behind them. He wasn't seriously listening to whatever the men had to say—it wasn't anything different from what he'd already heard.

People will know.

Something is wrong.

He makes the calls.

Vaslav tried to focus on the short bursts of his breaths as his wild gaze scanned the large portrait paintings of ballerinas. It was getting too bright again.

He didn't know where that light spilled in from. All the same, he couldn't bear it. The pain was back.

Vaslav shrunk into the first set of shadows he could find, and squeezed his eyes shut when his back hit a wall.

"Vas!" he heard someone call.

But he couldn't speak again.

Not when the stabbing bursts from the scattered migraine pain began to flutter, and he could barely hold himself up.

Footsteps raced by mere feet from his presence, beyond the sliver of light offered by a small doorway that he probably could have reached for if only his arms would do what he wanted them to.

"Vas—boss!"

"Where did he go?"

"*Vaslav!*"

*

Beep.
Beep.
BEEP.

Every one of those strange digital beeps accompanied a rocking motion that made Vaslav acutely aware of the fact his back was flat against something hard.

"Is the blinking a good sign?"

The question didn't get answered in the way the person likely wanted considering as soon as Vaslav had some sense of consciousness, he was fighting.

Ripping at the mask on his face, gasping in a burning lungful of air, he didn't recognize the faces of the men dressed in blue and white hovering over him. Roaring his anger and confusion out with flailing arms that sent everyone inching back.

But not for long.

Why was he laying down?

"Sir—"

"Sir, if you don't stop we'll have to tranq you!"

He might have laughed at that threat, but he was too busy shouting unintelligible curses. Tranq him? He'd have their hearts cut out and the blood in the chambers boiled for *tea*. Hadn't Igor just asked him a question?

Wasn't he in a dark room?

"Vas, *come on*."

"Give it, then," came the order.

"Twenty milligrams of—"

Good God.

Did they have him strapped down to a *gurney*?

His struggle increased at the same time a paramedic plunged a needle full of *something* straight into Vaslav's neck.

The beeping and rocking came back as his gaze settled on the glass window on the rear door of the vehicle. He couldn't see the faces of the three men anymore—not the two working on him or the one trying to stay out of their way, tucked into the rear corner.

He just saw the glass.

That's what the window made him remember.

What he saw first.

The glass.

When he had stumbled into the doorway with shadows, then down the dark hallway that he thought would save him from further pain in his confusion, he hadn't realized it had only been something of an alternative exit. It led him to a gallery, but he'd ignored the carpeted benches and tight stairwell that led downward for the wall of glass windows waiting in front of him.

He found something there. That's why he remembered the windows.

What was it?

*

"You can't be serious!"

Vaslav didn't even bother to dignify Igor's indignant outburst with a reply as he worked on buttoning up his silk shirt before reaching for his phone that someone had left on the portable stand next to the hospital bed.

"Tell him that he's crazy!"

"Well," the doctor started.

Vaslav passed the man standing in the hospital room doorway a look, but otherwise, didn't pay him any more mind. The last eighteen hours had not been easy for the doctor on a twenty-four-hour shift, never mind the ward's nurses. Vaslav was not at all a model patient and made every test and interaction far more difficult than it needed to be for everyone involved.

Without even trying, really.

Some might call it a talent.

"Well, *what?*" Igor barked at the man. "You just spent fifteen minutes explaining what *might* have caused his delirious episode, including that it could have been a mini stroke your tests didn't find, and now you're just going to allow him to walk out of here?"

"*He* is choosing to discharge himself, actually," the doctor replied calmly, "and considering the trouble he has already put this entire ward through since his arrival—including *your* demands for total secrecy while he was a patient, Mr. Ivanov—I am not left with very many options."

While the hallway outside of Vaslav's private room appeared quiet and empty, he seriously doubted that it was. Igor might have managed to keep anyone important from finding out about his sudden admittance to the hospital, but that did nothing for the people who found him *inside*.

He was a well-known figure in Moscow.

His name came with warnings.

As private as the doctor and nurses assigned to him had promised they would be, he trusted *no one*. Absolutely none of them. And he refused to remain within these walls for any longer than he had to.

They could not force him to say, so he was going. It was as simple as that.

"Listen," the doctor told Igor while Vaslav made his way around the suite to pick up his remaining belongings that had been scattered throughout the space over the last night and day. "Medically, he's clear. There are no more neurological symptoms, his pain is back down to a manageable scale, and there isn't any immediate intervention he needs or that we could justifiably do. Yes, we could run more tests, but—"

"So can my other doctors," Vaslav murmured.

The man in the white lab coat sighed. "Exactly. I'm sorry; less stress, let him relax. There isn't much else I can do here."

"*B'lyad.*"

Igor's cuss flew over the doctor's head as the man turned on his heel and left without a word. There wasn't anything else that needed to be said, honestly. Vaslav probably wouldn't even waste the time it would take to sign the discharge papers at the front desk.

"You were right, the week was too much," he said to his head of security. Igor's behavior came from his worry, and Vaslav understood that but in the end … he made the final call. *Every call.* Especially on this. "I should have just taken an early weekend when I woke up already wanting to puke."

Igor sighed, scrubbing a tattooed hand over his bald head before he said, "I called Nico. He's coming back from his trip early."

That didn't make Vaslav any happier. Not that he thought Igor suspected it would. Nico left the country with unfinished business between him and his boss, and that was already a problem. His sovietnik still had things to answer for regarding Feliks and The Swan House. At least, the hours spent at the hospital weren't entirely wasted.

He had time to think.

To remember.

The incident that found him here wasn't enough to divert his plans entirely. It only put them off for a short while.

"Good," he said to a quiet Igor. "Make sure the first person he comes to see when he steps off that plane is me, yes?"

Igor nodded. "You won't even give them one more night, Vas? Just to check or—"

"There's nothing to find."

And even if there was, Vaslav couldn't say he wanted to know.

Clearly seeing he wasn't going to get anywhere with Vaslav, certainly not when it came to convincing him that the hospital was where he needed to be, Igor headed for the door. "I'll call the driver and get the car ready. For the record, nobody knows you're here; nobody will."

Vaslav didn't look away from the rings he slid back into place on his fingers, or the watch he affixed to his thick wrist as he muttered, "Perfect—I'd hate to have to kill both my spies for being totally fucking incompetent."

"Boss—"

"There was a woman."

Igor froze in the doorway, shooting a look over his shoulder at Vaslav who was lost to his thoughts again. He'd been doing that a lot since his consciousness came back, and the confusion finally cleared. This place gave him too much time to think, and he hated that just as much as he despised the idea that someone might think something was wrong with him.

"Pardon?" Igor asked.

Vaslav considered not repeating his question—it meant admitting maybe his memory wasn't entirely back like he'd claimed when the doctor had done a simple neurological test before agreeing to his discharge demand.

That didn't change what he knew.

Or what Igor might know, for that matter.

"She was dancing below the gallery," Vaslav said, choosing each word carefully. The same way he chose what he would not say. That he remembered placing his hands along the ledge where the glass wall was so that he could watch the woman dance in her tights and sneakers. Or how when she finished, coming out of a fouetté, she'd been crying.

All at once, the music that had been playing on her phone silenced and left the dark studio down below heavy. Even through the glass, though she hadn't known then that he was watching her, Vaslav had *felt* it.

Her heaviness—the sadness—it permeated.

He didn't know what had made her look up and see him there, but when she did, he'd collapsed again. Apparently, the small stairwell he'd noticed when he made his way into the gallery room led downstairs to the studio.

He'd heard every one of her racing steps up to find him, and how loud she had screamed for help.

While the unknown woman touched his face, still tear-streaked from her own private breakdown, she'd asked him for his name. She'd not been concerned by

36

the grisly scar that her fingertips grazed as she maintained their eye contact. Even when she yelled for help a third and fourth time, her blue eyes had never once looked away from his own.

Vaslav hadn't given her his name. All he remembered asking back was, "Why were you crying?"

That was how Igor and Feliks managed to find where he'd wandered off to down the corridor. Because the woman had been there to help.

Vaslav never got an answer about her tears; he also didn't get her name.

But he remembered her.

"The woman in the gallery," Vaslav said, turning to face Igor fully in the hospital room. "The one that found me—who is she?"

"A ballerina for the company, I suspect."

"*Yes*, but which one?"

Igor's gaze narrowed a bit. "Do you want me to find out?"

Even he could hear the way the man's sarcasm bled into the question—just enough to say he thought Vaslav's current focus, considering he probably shouldn't even be getting discharged, was skewed. Didn't he have better things to worry about than an unknown woman who danced ballet in sneakers and only felt like a fragment in his memories?

Sure, he did.

And still, Vaslav couldn't stop himself when he said, "Find her for me. I want to know who she is."

He could figure out why later.

5.

Vera swore under her breath as she almost knocked over the potted orchid waiting at the front doorstep of her Noble Row villa. It was the peek of a familiar script on the card that had been hung from the stem held up by a stick that made her smile, though.

Bending down, and leaving her door still cracked for her four-bedroom villa that she had bought shortly after her broken ankle was cleared, it was the first thing in her life that she dropped any real money on and then spent hours with an interior decorator making it exactly the place she wanted to call home. It felt like hers.

She recognized the script font her father always had the florist use whenever he called in to send her something special. Flipping the card over, a small note from Demyan was printed alongside the flower shop's logo.

Your mother said you sounded sad the other night. I hope this makes you smile. Love you, Vera. Call me if you want. -

Papa

Of course.

Demyan always added that little *if you want* on his messages, even when he called and left one for her voicemail because he'd learned long ago that Vera didn't like it when people pushed. She had been capable of making the right choices for herself from the time she was young; none she ever made steered her wrong.

They simply didn't always end the way she expected.

Tucking the potted orchid with its pretty purple and white petals onto the small table just inside her doorway, Vera closed and locked the villa. She lived with roommates, chosen by her father and her bodyguard at the time, initially when she first came to Russia, and then rented a more expensive, luxury apartment in the party district of Moscow with other girls from The Swan House after she turned eighteen. Her one roommate at that time, Hannah, moved out before she bought the villa.

Nothing quite suited her like the row of villas, yellow upon yellow, each featuring its own entrance, garage, and large terraces with views of the Kremlin. The fenced backyards leading to the walkways and park continuing through or back out of the community had been her favorite part, though. She'd never felt unsafe here—and Ostozhenka was a short fifteen-minute walk away from The Swan House, even if she only went there on a voluntary basis a couple of times a week. It was still close.

Like everything else she needed.

It meant she didn't need to bother with a car, which Vera liked considering driving in Russia was not like back home. Renting a vehicle was far easier whenever she had a need for doing so ... which honestly, wasn't often.

Pulling the cell phone from her crossbody bag, Vera dialed her father's familiar number as she took the front steps of the villa's stoop two at a time. Her neighbor, who was letting his dog piss while he watered the vines that crawled between their fenced yards, waved to her as she passed the view of his gate.

Demyan picked up her call on the fourth ring. "Sometimes I wonder if you even bother to look at the time."

Vera laughed. "I know what time it is there—six."

"Yes, in the morning."

"Are you saying you weren't already up?"

"Well."

Vera grinned wide at the amusement in her father's tone. He was caught. He could complain all the time about the time difference when she called, but if it was past five in the morning, the man was up. Sometimes, he didn't close his eyes before one.

"You got the orchid, then?"

"I did, thank you."

Demyan hummed, clearing his throat before he asked. "And did it make you smile?"

"You always make me smile, Papa."

"I try, anyway. Sometimes, you make it hard."

Or the distance did.

"I wasn't sad when Ma called," she said, "by the way."

Only after.

"She was pretty sure—"

"Claire worries. That's all. I was just lonely. Other people were busy, so I called her."

Demyan didn't reply right away which made Vera think he heard the lie in her words even though the cadence of her tone hadn't changed. She was still her cheerful, bright self but as hard as she tried to keep that demeanor and outlook, there was still something wrong inside.

She felt it there.

Thick, and heavy.

Right in the middle of her chest.

She just didn't know what.

"Hannah moved back to Italy last month, didn't she?" Demyan asked, referring to Vera's oldest, and last real friend that she could count on.

Well, used to.

Hannah remained in Moscow even after she retired from ballet two years ago because she'd met and married her husband, a man with high status in the Kremlin. Their divorce had been vicious and spectacular. It also chased her friend back to Italy where her mother, a former supermodel, waited to soften the blow once the ink was dry.

Vera hadn't blamed her.

They talked as often as they could.

"I have other friends here," Vera said before her father could go ahead and point out the obvious.

"Acquaintances, I think."

She sighed.

Demyan chuckled deeply on the other end of the phone, adding, "It's okay to say that a lot has changed in Moscow since you moved there ten years ago, Vera. Everything changes."

"I didn't say I wanted to leave."

"According to your mother, you don't have to."

"She just—"

"Worries," Demyan interjected. "Because she raised you from the time you barely reached her waist. Claire knows."

Part of Vera's issue with admitting life wasn't entirely roses and sunshine stemmed from the fact that she really didn't want her parents to concern themselves with her problems. They had enough to deal with between her younger, wild brother, Roman, who constantly found trouble wherever he went, and her father's business that constantly kept him on the radar of men who either wanted him dead … or behind bars.

Vera could take care of herself.

And once she figured out what she needed to make her smiles real again, then she would do it. Her parents couldn't help with that.

"Tell Ma I love her," Vera said.

"Hey, you're not letting me go already, are you?"

"I have a class today."

Every Monday, Thursday, and Saturday, actually. Two weeks a month. The other two, the schedule rotated to Monday, Wednesday, and Friday.

"Yes, in a couple of hours. I know your routine better than even you, I'm sure."

From all the way across the world, too.

Vera wished she was surprised.

"I'm having a late lunch with Feliks, actually."

That earned her a displeased grunt from her father. "That prick—"

"Yeah, I know."

Demyan didn't say anything more, his disgust bleeding through his silence into the phone. Vera didn't really need him to vocalize his feelings because she already knew how little he cared for the man that owned the ballet company she was not entirely ready to leave.

"It's not a lunch like that," she said quickly.

Not a date, she meant.

"Good." Her father scoffed, muttering, "Can't see what you'd want with him, though. He stays out of your business well enough, doesn't he? I can make sure my next message to the piece of shit makes it clear about exactly where we all stand here."

"Let's just say we have an agreement."

For now, it worked.

If she only had to deal with Feliks when absolutely necessary, her presence remained at The Swan House in some capacity that helped the company. Like being the face of the free ballet studio and lessons offered to the underprivileged kids, getting them through a door that they otherwise would never see.

Vera had other things on her mind where Feliks and the lunch meeting was concerned. She'd only needed to see him fucking a young woman bent over his desk once to know the man would stick his dick in anything that was wet between her thighs if he could. He hadn't even apologized considering Vera had still been wearing the ballgown for the event that they had been meant to attend that night when she walked in on her boyfriend of three months cheating on her.

No, she didn't want Feliks. And the asshole knew he'd never touch her again.

"Don't give the cocksucker an inch, Vera," Demyan told her. "Whatever your little lunch is for ... not a single goddamn inch. It'll be public, right?"

"Yep, right by the windows." She smiled, though her father couldn't see it. "Don't worry—he's always needed me way more than I ever needed him."

Even now.

The bastard probably couldn't forget it, either.

"That's my girl."

*

Vera had already ordered and was halfway through her black Russian grilled cheese sandwich and lemonade by the time Feliks decided to show up at the restaurant. Not particularly known for its fanfare, the small family-owned eatery offered some of her favorite treats from simple bread to traditional desserts that she couldn't find anywhere else.

At least, not ones that tasted the same.

Lucky for her, the teal and salmon decorated restaurant was located directly in the middle between her villa and The Swan House. Which meant Feliks had no good excuse to be late, but he was just the same.

Sliding into the booth where she sat, Feliks didn't give her a second glance before he reached for the menu placed between two matryoshka dolls that doubled as salt and pepper shakers. Their booth sat next to the large bay windows overlooking the section of the eatery where patrons could eat outside at tables under umbrellas. Just beyond, the busy street never stopped moving with vehicles and a small crowd crossing a crosswalk.

"That looks good," Feliks noted, nodding at her grilled cheese.

"Brie cheese, black forest ham, and—"

"I only needed to know the cheese." Feliks' hand raised at the waitress passing by the table next to their booth. He pointed at Vera's plate, saying his order in

Russian to the woman, "What she's had—but do me a solid and make the cider hard."

"*Da srazu—yes, right away*," the blonde responded with a brilliant smile before tucking her hands into the matching pink apron of her uniform and heading for the kitchen.

"You still like this place?"

Small talk, now?

Well, Vera couldn't blame Feliks, she supposed. The last real conversation the two had ended with her threatening to stab her house keys into his ball sack if he showed up at her place drunk again. That had been a couple of years ago. They only spoke now when he wanted to confirm that she didn't need a schedule change.

"Who wouldn't?" she asked back.

Feliks only grunted in reply, but his gaze turned away from her to the window and the activity outside. "I thought we weren't doing this anymore. You and me ... whatever we're doing here."

"We're not, but it's a hell of a lot better than someone seeing me step foot near your office."

He tipped his head a bit to the side at that, giving her a view of the tattoo that disappeared somewhere beneath the collar of his dress shirt. Always unbuttoned at the throat and one down his chest. He liked to draw women's gazes, but hers had already been fine-tuned to this man.

He didn't interest her anymore. His allure quickly faded the first time a woman realized he really was just a selfish bastard out for his own gain. Even ugly could be beautiful.

"So, you asked me to lunch for what, then?"

"Well, my lunch is almost done," Vera replied.

"Don't apologize for being late, I really don't care."

Raising his brow, he glanced over at her. If he didn't like her tone, he chose not to voice it, but his stare was more than enough. Too bad for him.

"Well—"

"The man, last Thursday," she said, talking before he could ask something else, she wouldn't bother to entertain. "I just wanted to ask if he was okay."

For a few seconds, Feliks expression didn't change although his gaze darted back to the window all the same. That didn't stop Vera from seeing the way he scanned the outside movement, giving himself time to think before he asked, "What were you doing, anyway?"

That time, it was Vera's turn to blink away her surprise. "I had a class."

"The studio was empty, and mostly dark. The kids had all gone. I didn't notice the exact time, but we have cameras, I could easily—"

"You know I dance sometimes after. Alone."

Clearing his throat at that admission, Feliks only nodded.

Vera let out a hard breath, adding, "I saw him fall in the upper gallery, and ran to help. Right time, right place is all. Nobody else knew anything about it, and he kind of seemed out of it. I've been worried about it."

About *him*.

It had all been amazingly fast and chaotic. Vera barely had her hands on the stranger's scarred face before Feliks and another man had heard her shouting for help. Before they'd rushed in, though, the stranger asked her something she hadn't been able to forget—*why were you crying?*

She didn't even have the time to think about the fact that the man had been watching her dance, never mind asking his name. The men who rushed to help him quickly brushed Vera off, even as they helped the man stand and led him out of the gallery through the rear exit hallway.

Who knew what happened after? Her hands shook for the rest of the night because she couldn't get the stranger's face out of her mind every time, she closed her eyes. In just a few seconds, she had memorized the lines that spoke of age around his icy blue eyes and the frightening clarity that watched her.

He'd not really been able to move. His gaze had jumped wildly back and forth, and the grimace that had been set into his mouth while he lay on the floor had told her that he'd been in pain.

Was he okay now?

"*It's fine, he's fine*," Feliks had snapped at Vera in the gallery that evening.

But it wasn't.

Except long ago, Vera had learned her place in The Swan House. Sometimes, men came and went from the halls who did not like to be questioned or known. They were the same kind of men who let the tattoos on their body be their only warning for others to stay away.

Often, it was better to just do as one was told.

So, last Thursday, she had.

"I only want to know if he's okay," she explained to Feliks who had finally turned to look at her again. "You know how I am; I overthink everything and—"

"If you know what's good for you," Feliks replied, his tone cold and hard, "you'll never ask about that man again. And you won't stay later than you're supposed to at the studio from here on out, Vera. I hope that's clear."

He didn't give her the option to respond before he stood from the booth, dropped money to the table, and walked away without a look back.

So much for lunch.

"I only wanted to know if he was okay!" she called as Feliks shoved through the small restaurant's front doors.

His response was the door swinging shut, and Vera desperately wished she could go back to her meal without the curious patrons now staring at her.

Damn.

6.

Vera.

Appropriate for a woman with the face of an angel, Vaslav thought, considering the name meant faith. Twenty-six. Born on December first in a New York hospital to a mother that died days after her birth.

Her family ties were certainly … interesting. He had to wonder if the person who handed Vera an invitation to the infamous house of ballet in Moscow realized her connections to the New York mob.

Or rather, her father's.

Vera Giana Avdonin.

He wasn't at all surprised to learn that she had been practicing ballet from almost the time she could walk considering her ties to The Swan House. She never would have walked through those doors had she not been worthy.

Moscow, it seemed, was where the young woman's life really began.

And possibly ended, in a way.

That was where things became interesting for Vaslav as he flipped through the file of information that Igor had delivered the morning before. As he wasn't particularly a Monday person, he didn't bother to indulge his curiosity about the woman who very well might have saved his life on that gallery floor until now.

Who knew how long it might have taken Feliks or Igor to find him had she not been a witness to his fall? A similar fall at the hospital had led the doctor to an interesting—or frightening—discovery that Vaslav hadn't been able to forget.

"Something happened when he was on the floor—his blood pressure dropped to practically nothing. Had he been down just a couple of minutes more, well ..."

Vaslav shook off the doctor's observations that just wouldn't leave the back of his mind. Like everything else that had been said, or given as a warning, during his stay at the hospital; it was easier to ignore what he saw as a problem that couldn't be fixed.

"You've seen it all, then?"

"Working on it," he replied to Igor.

An easy lie.

He'd been through the file.

"It would have been easier, and faster probably, had she not been from the states."

"Right, right." His distracted murmur went unanswered that time. Not that he cared.

Vaslav didn't even bother to glance up from the file on the desk he liked to keep in the den to properly greet Igor as he stepped further inside the space. While the walls of white plaster trimmed with gold flake and mahogany bookshelves in his larger office smelled like the cigars he'd once enjoyed frequently—

although now, they only flared his migraines—the den on the bottom level of his three-level Federal Colonial-style mansion was where he chose to spend more time.

It was darker.

Fewer windows.

The floor got so cold in the evenings that it gave him some relief when he was desperate enough to get down on it and press his forehead or cheek to the shiny, cherry oak hardwood. If anyone ever caught him, he always said he was praying.

Who dared to call him out on the lie?

The flat screen television that took up a good portion of one wall was turned on only to watch the news or monitor his outdoor security cameras. There were none inside the house. He slept on the rose-colored couch beside the matching chair and loveseat that sat in the middle of the room meant for conversation more often than he didn't.

Connected to the rear of the den was a hallway that led to a bathroom on the left and a small stairwell on the right that could take him straight up to his master bedroom through a private door. There was a separate entrance and exit, and guns hidden behind the molding of every shelf. Even a safe was built into a cement box beneath the section of floor in front of his desk where a Persian rug and a set of chairs kept it hidden. What else did he need?

Vaslav sometimes even found peace in here.

"There's quite a bit of information once she was here, yes?"

Vaslav rubbed his tongue along the edge of his front teeth, sucking in air before replying, "I can see that."

He didn't offer anything else because Igor likely already knew every piece of information inside the file. No doubt, he'd take his time to flip through the images of the sixteen-year-old ballerina who had been on the cusp of being practically a public figure from the moment she stepped foot on Russian soil.

She'd been featured in magazines. Perfect to the public and loved by the city. A star by the time she was eighteen.

The newspaper images of her in costume, on a stage or for promo, were not good enough for his liking, but he didn't say that out loud. He bet she'd received the culture shock of her life on top of being a teenager while being given freedom and a life like few others would ever have or experience. Never mind at that age.

Yet, she never even stumbled. The pressure never got to her, or so it seemed on paper. Laid out like this, like a puzzle that wasn't complete, Vera became all too interesting to Vaslav.

"You're sure this was her—she's the one?" Vaslav asked.

Igor shrugged. "Apparently so. The gallery was part of the studio they use for her free classes to poor children. That wasn't too hard to find. I didn't even need to go to Feliks for that. It's only her affiliation that even gains the place any donations."

Right.

Because The Swan House hadn't done anything meaningful in the world of ballet since the disaster that had been their final showing of what had been called *In the Stars*. According to what Vaslav had already learned from his file. Igor didn't know it, and his boss wouldn't offer the information, but Vaslav had already rifled through each document, image and even the thin USB card at the back. In fact, if he turned on the television that he'd connected through to his laptop on the desk, Vera Avdonin would still be mid-air on the screen. Ready to fall straight down through a latch door that would have been opened in the middle of the stage as she finished the scene with what was known as a fouetté arabesque jump.

One might think a trick like that would be *well* practiced. Timing would have needed to be impeccable, no room for error. He believed it probably was because they'd run the ballet for months with guests flying in from all over the world, but on the last time, the door apparently didn't open in time.

A man on the crew had been later blamed, and unsurprisingly, fired. Then, he put a bullet to his head and quietly washed-up dead in the canal. *Quietly*, because there hadn't even been a paper printed about it, only a notice of death by the family.

If Vaslav turned on that TV, and pressed play by hitting the enter key on his laptop, Igor would see that he'd already watched the moment when Vera had shattered her ankle in front of thousands before falling through the floor like she had been meant to all along. From every angle that had apparently been recorded that night.

He had little to no interest in discussing the puzzle he had already put together himself from the information Igor provided.

Igor took the unspoken hint from his boss before he raised a brow when Vaslav offered nothing else, asking him, "Are you satisfied, then? Hell, you even have her current address."

"*Hmm.*"

"God, what?"

Fiddling with the onyx oval ring set in a twenty-four-karat gold band around his middle finger, Vaslav took another glance at the stack of papers he would soon burn about Vera Avdonin. Some of it, he hadn't given as much focus as he had others—like her nightlife in Moscow, and the rumors the rags had printed as she was on the cusp of her womanhood.

That time was long gone for her, he bet. Youthful abandon quickly became a thing of the past when in seconds, life-changing moments stopped someone right in their path. That type of thing had a way of making a person rethink everything.

Still, from the newspaper shot of her waving from the private jet that had flew her into Moscow for the first time, to the one showcasing her behind a row of preteen girls all in matching tights and leotards that was taken only a year earlier, her smile never changed. The fact she was pleasing to look at didn't hurt.

She was a classic beauty—every image, even the grainy ones—allowed him to appreciate that. Almond-shaped blue eyes and almost-black hair that she had always kept long until her accident.

After that, she'd sheared it off for a bob. One that accentuated the angular line of her jaw and small chin. Every picture left her looking doll-like. Perfect, maybe air-brushed milk and cream skin, small heart-shaped pink lips. Even her tiny nose with a thin bridge and not a freckle in sight was turned up ever so slightly at the tip so that she had one of *those* faces.

An expression even when she was still. One that seemed to stare right out at someone, or through them, without even trying.

"Vas," Igor said.

He still didn't bother to look away from the scattered papers and images even as his man came into the line of his vision just beyond the edge of the desk.

"Why would she stay after all that?" Leaning forward on his elbows, Vaslav used the tips of his thumbs to press against his chin while his fingers wove over top each other. "She can't dance," he added even as the image of Vera twirling across a glossy hardwood floor of a dimly lit studio filled his mind. "I doubt her popularity is anywhere near what it was before. Her family rarely visits, although … we don't have to wonder why there."

Or he didn't, anyway.

A non-traditional bratva boss from the western world who held no connection to his motherland or the *vory* who made his position possible … Well, that wasn't exactly welcomed here.

"What does it matter?" Igor asked. "All she did was find you on the floor."

Igor wasn't wrong, but nobody ever said Vaslav was rational, either. If people predicted his strange compulsions and obsessions, or even his violence, would he be where he was today? He didn't think so.

He rarely ever questioned his own curiosity— something else that had accompanied him since he was a child. It was that same sense of wanting to know and needing to solve the problem in front of him that had often steered him on paths that changed his life. Not always for the better, but he'd never been one to complain about that.

"I could look further into it," Igor started to say, though the slow way he spoke the words suggested he'd rather not feed into Vaslav's newest puzzle.

"Actually, I think I might ask her myself," Vaslav said, finally glancing up to meet the stoic gaze of Igor, "once I find the time."

"What do you—"

"Where the fuck is Nico?"

Igor hadn't expected the sudden question if the way he rocked back on his heels before stilling on the spot was any indication. *Good.* It was always best to keep people on guard.

"As far as I—"

"*As far as you know*," Vaslav mocked, happy he'd earned a wince from the towering man. "Just tell me where he fucking is!"

"Arrived back on Sunday night. I told him to give it a couple of days."

"I told him to be here the second his feet touched the goddamn tarmac!"

"You didn't even crawl out of bed until early Monday morning. I know, I called Mira every hour."

Vaslav's teeth grinded at the mention of his only servant. The woman had worked for his mother for years, and now edging toward her sixties, she stayed at the estate because *he* asked her to. The woman knew what he liked—his mother didn't give a shit as long as a floor was clean and her sheets were fresh.

He wasn't quite the same.

"Get him here," Vaslav said. "*Tonight*, Igor, or else you'll lose fingers this time."

"I only wanted to give you time, boss."

Glaring at the man, he asked, "Time for what?"

"To think, maybe. Talk first, shoot second."

Smirking from his left side, Vaslav shook his head and twirled a finger over the file and mess of papers on his desk, drawing Igor's gaze that way. "You see, I did think … I've learned quite a lot. And none of it matters because Nico still did what he did when he gave an Abramov money from the bank account of one of my men. *No matter* the man."

Even his closest spy.

That was not how this business worked.

"Get him here," he ordered one last time.

Igor nodded, and didn't say another word before he took his leave without being dismissed. Vaslav honestly didn't mind.

Not three minutes after his head of security could be seen walking off the security camera at the front door on the television he'd turned on the second Igor left, Vaslav switched the scene back to show what was still on pause on his laptop.

Vera in mid-air.

At the height of her career.

A second from failure.

What had that moment felt like?

Was that why she'd been crying?

"Mr. Pashkov?"

Vas cleared his throat as his gaze cut away from the screen to the woman leaning in the doorway of the den. Her flat gray uniform with a basic white apron and sensible black shoes gave away her place to anyone who stepped inside his residence. Yet, he always demanded people respect Mira. Her life had not been an easy one, yet she was dedicated and loyal to Vaslav and his family. What little he had left.

She deserved respect for that, at the very least. After all, she was the only left living within these walls alongside him and dealing with his bullshit certainly wasn't a trip to the spa … even if she did stay well hidden and out of his way most of the time.

"What?" he asked roughly, scrubbing a hand over his itching scar and beard. He needed more of the oil he liked that worked to soften both.

"Natalia rang through."

Something stuck to his throat at the news of his mother's call, but he forced the irritation back. He'd always had an interesting and volatile relationship with the woman who had given him both life and the last name that belonged to her father. As far as he understood, she'd never known which client had been his.

"What did she want?" he asked.

Mira was already slinking back beyond the door, her words echoing behind her. "To visit. Tea tonight."

Perfect fucking timing.

7.

Vaslav could chop a cord of wood in an hour or so if he had a good momentum going. One of the only forms of exercise he enjoyed, it also served more purpose than just his physical state. The large house, including the smaller guest lodge with three bedrooms at the far end of the property—a smaller copy, designed to look like a miniature version of the estate's real house—used wood in multiple furnaces that had been vented throughout the many floors to stay warm.

While he didn't need much wood currently, it never hurt to chop a cord and throw it down into the massive cellar where he—or someone else—could pile it up for later use. Wood burned better the longer it sat, anyway.

Nonetheless, if his mood happened to be decent and his pain level was manageable, a visitor would likely find Vaslav out back, lost in the rhythmic *woosh* of his axe cutting through air and the *clunk-clunk* of chopped wood falling into a pile around the stump he used to hold the current block.

"There you are," Vaslav heard called as he set up his next piece of wood. His mother's tone was already too shrill for his liking.

Natalia Pashkova was a yeller—the more animated or angry she became, the worse she shrieked—and his level of tolerance was typically determined by how drunk she was at any given moment. It was the only thing she did well, considering her temper was nearly as legendary as his own, and truth be told, he'd learned it first at home.

"Why on earth are we having tea out here now?"

"Because it makes your presence slightly more bearable, *Mat*."

Only partly, he added silently. When he wasn't confined—with her, that shit made him edgy.

Natalia hadn't heard her son's insult as she stepped down from the rear veranda and headed his way on the cobblestone path. He considered repeating it just because he didn't care whether she knew his feelings or not about her presence that evening but opted for the less stressful option.

"The weather is beautiful," he told her when she came to drop ungraciously into the rattan sofa where it faced a massive brick fireplace big enough to burn a body and the rest of the rear property. "Why wouldn't I want to be outside? The sun hasn't even set yet."

Soon, though.

Within the hour.

Then, things would get interesting.

Natalia's gaze cut toward the house when a door opened and closed. Mira quickly came into view carrying a tray filled with anything and everything they might need to keep his mother happy for her teatime.

Vaslav went back to chopping wood while Mira handled his mother.

"Still won't tell me who makes these teas?" Natalia asked while her teacup was filled with boiling water from the fine China teapot where his favorite coconut and berry tea had been steeping for a minimum of ten minutes.

Just the way he liked it.

There was something about the smell of the coconut mixed with berries that calmed him in a way few other things did. Not that he would ever admit as much.

Whether the question was for him, he opted not to answer. Mira was there to save the day, but he knew it wouldn't be long before she made herself scarce.

"A man in Ontario makes the bags and sends them once a month," Mira explained. "You know I only steep the tea for Mr. Pashkov, Miss Natalia."

"Yes, but maybe I would like to have some—"

"NiagraTeas," Vaslav said in a grunt while the axe slicing through a massive chunk of wood at the same time. As the blocks fell to the ground, he sent his axe flying into the stump where it remained stuck as he turned to face his mother. "I'm sure the company would be happy to make you some tea, *Mat.*"

Natalia, with her legs crossed under the skirt of her flower-printed summer dress, was already lifting the teacup to her pursed lips for a taste. She still liked her button-up cardigans, too, and matching them with the color of her outfit. She paused, tapping the pointed toe of her stiletto heels against nothing but air, just long enough to say, "See, that wasn't so hard, was it?"

Vaslav seriously considered heading for the house

at that comment—no doubt, his mother was just getting started with her snide comments and thinly veiled displeasure. When he was young, he blamed her lack of empathy and cruel ways on her drinking and upbringing. The only man worse than both combined, after all, was her own father.

A man whose name they no longer spoke.

"What do you want?" he outright asked.

Natalia let out a little sigh and sipped from her tea. Mira quickly finished her business, not speaking to mother or son, including pouring Vaslav's cup, before making her way to the house without another look back.

"What makes you think I want anything?" Natalia asked back, raising one perfectly manicured eyebrow as if to defy her son's accusation.

One wouldn't guess by looking at Natalia Pashkova that she had turned sixty-three that year. Oh, he'd been told the bash was epic—there were even fireworks over Moscow. The beloved socialite that had never quite let go of the party. He'd never met someone quite as vain as her, and even when he was only five, and she, twenty-two, he could remember her staring at her mostly naked body in the mirror and blaming him for the tiny white stripes that were barely visible on her thighs.

"*You're the only one I kept, you know?*" she would tell him a few years later after he'd discovered through the older boys in the neighborhood who'd teased him about it why so many men came and went with her. "*Papasha was dead then, he didn't have a say anymore. I shouldn't have kept you, either. Look what you did to me.*"

One of many fond memories.

"I haven't even been around since the beginning of

June," his mother lamented.

"Mmm," Vaslav grunted back. "Because your allowance showed up right on time, and with a little bit extra, no?"

There was a split second between the delivery of his words and how his mother's face twitched ever-so-slightly. The Botox did wonders, or so he was told. She didn't look a day over forty, and he had more gray peppered into his dark temples than she did.

Nonetheless, he'd seen her flinch.

The *almost*-scowl.

Yet, in seconds she was smiling in that *whatever-you-like-dear* way of hers that had his fucking skin crawling.

"Vas," she practically cooed.

Natalia even waved her coffin-shaped blood-red nails his way.

"Mat."

"Why so formal?"

Good God, she tested every ounce of his patience. The second he sighed, giving her the reaction—*any reaction;* that was the problem—she wanted, Natalia pounced.

In her own special way.

"Just say it—*Mother, the reason I've sent you more money, and will keep doing so, is to keep you far away from me. Agree?"* Natalia shrugged, laughing under her breath as she stood from the sofa, her gaze still locked on him. What bothered him the most about his mother were her eyes. They matched his. Icy blue, practically dead, and entirely genetic. They were more alike than either of them would admit. Setting her teacup to the matching rattan table, she said, "I mean, then we wouldn't have to go through all these theatrics."

"You don't want to be here anyway."

"That's not the point!"

Oh, wonderful.

The yelling had started.

Vaslav simply didn't have the patience for it. "Knock it off, *Mat.*"

It was the tone he used that got his point across. Flat, but full of bass. *Booming*, she told him when he started puberty at a young eleven and nearly shot up past six feet tall overnight. Her swatting stopped, then. She never reached for a belt—or anything else she liked to beat him with, broom handles included—again when she was scared that he might hit back. By then, however, it was already too late. A too-young Vaslav had stumbled on a gang of boys that were his size but had a few years on his.

Everything went downhill after that.

She'd never cared enough to save him, anyway.

Sometimes, he could deal with her bullshit. The shrieking and going on; her drunk episodes in the city that required a clean-up, usually by financial means; and all the other nonsense she had put him through ever since she learned he'd found measurable success after prison.

Well, then it had been easier.

But not so much, now.

His time felt too precious.

Natalia sucked in a sharp breath, squeezing her lips together while her blonde hair blew with the wind, and she tried to stare him down. "You can't *abuse* me—"

"Who's abused, *suka?*"

"You little *prick!*"

Vaslav fell into the chair on the left side of the sofa,

folding his hands over his chest while he chuckled. He took great satisfaction folding one leather shoe over his knee and staring up at the woman who had never once shown him an ounce of love or gratefulness for all he'd suffered through for her, yet still demanded more.

Especially when he'd pissed her off.

"Who's little, *Mat?*"

That shut her up instantly.

He let her fume where she stood while he eyed the darkening sky.

"So, that's it, then?" Natalia asked.

"Extra every month as long as I don't see your face more than once."

"*Fine by me.*"

Vas smirked at that, tipping his head to the side so his mother could see beyond the scarred profile he previously offered. "And that includes any issues I might have to *hear* about."

At that news, he could almost see her face fall. But that decade-old face lift and her constant use of Botox kept it firmly in place.

He respected her dedication if nothing else.

"But ... Vas—"

"*Mat*, it's not up for discussion. Believe it or not, I don't actually have the time to chase after you anymore, and the one or two men I have tasked with dealing with you over the years have both made it clear it's pointless. Learn a different way, now."

Natalia tossed her arms high, shouting at him, "You wouldn't have *any* of this if it wasn't for me!"

He almost laughed at that, but she hadn't quite pissed him off enough yet to earn it. "Still can't believe how fast you blew through the ten million roubles I paid for this place."

She'd been all too gleeful, and greedy, to sign those papers.

"Oh, *fuck you*," she spat at him in Russian.

Vaslav only smiled.

She didn't deny it, though.

The fact that he was now able to control his mother's purse strings—because the nearly twenty years of his life dedicated to the oath he spoke for his brotherhood allowed him all his blessings—worked to his favor more often than it didn't.

He didn't blame her, really.

Forced to grow up too young, cruelty was in her blood, and she'd passed that poison right to him. She never should have been a mother; he'd been sent to prison for fifteen years trying to prove he was a good son.

Their time, whenever it was that they could have been what each other needed, was *long* over.

"Whatever," Natalia spat, turning on her heels and rounding the arm of the sofa to head for the back of the large house.

Vaslav didn't move. "Say goodbye to Nico on your way out."

It would likely be the last time she did.

At that, she paused.

"You won't kill him."

He was the one who decided to wait to respond that time. Vaslav was far from stupid, and he knew what she was doing. *Fishing.* For information likely, because the less time she spent in her son's vicinity or home meant the more she had to pry information out of others. It was just her way; woven into her nature as a means of survival.

It's why he couldn't trust her.

Or anyone, really.

There was only one person—besides Igor, and that bastard wouldn't go within five meters of Natalia if he weren't forced to—who might have overheard certain things regarding his recent displeasure with Nico.

The air that slipped past his lips was the only cold thing besides his heart, but he needed that breath to chill the next words he spoke.

"You're wrong," he replied, "and stop manipulating information out of Mira. It takes more of my energy than I care to spend playing your fucking games, Natalia."

There.

He'd dropped the *mat* entirely. Vaslav wouldn't even call her mother, if that's what would get her the hell out of his face at this point.

Over her shoulder, her hard gaze locked into his. She lifted one shoulder, saying only, "No you won't. He's been your best friend for fifteen years; stood beside you when you married Irina. Had the bitch birthed you any bastards, he would have been there for that, too."

Pain unfolded in Vaslav's chest.

Like the tentacles of a sea monster exploding from his heart and wrapping his entire torso in a tight, heavy agony that he couldn't escape, the pain was instant, vicious, and he hated Natalia for it.

The physical pain was one thing. He'd been dealing with that for years. Every so often, though, that emotional trauma living inside the crater that had once been his heart released its brokenness to the rest of him.

Death would be kinder.

Goddamn his mother for knowing that button, and for pushing it every fucking time.

"Last warning," Vaslav said, his flat affect never once wavering while his gaze zeroed in on the far line of the property where it melted into a climbing hill of trees, and a laugh began to crawl its way out of his chest. "Talk about her to me ever again—to anyone, *Mat*—and I will have you burned to death on the steps of the Kremlin while the whole city watches."

He didn't turn to see the expression on her face, but the answering silence said it all. Only that small breeze remained until the sounds of Natalia's footsteps started to creep away.

He did not make threats he would not see through.

One last time, she would light up the city.

Push me, Vaslav thought.

Natalia kept walking instead.

"Like I said," he called after her before she could no longer hear, "say hi to Nico."

8.

It was a quarter past nine before the pat-pat of footsteps on the cobblestone path broke through Vaslav's concentration once more. Despite his mother's unwelcome visit, he still managed to make through almost an entire cord of wood from what remained in his log pile. He'd have to get the young men from last summer back on the property with their machines to cut and haul a few trees from the rear property again.

Another task completed.

Something else he wouldn't have to worry about.

Vaslav wondered what the point was, now.

"How was your trip?" he asked, spinning on his booted heels to face his new companion.

Nico fell into the chair facing the one Vaslav was heading for as he finally laid his gaze on his sovietnik. Slumped in the rattan chair with his hand resting along his cheek, his friend only stared back but said nothing.

"You don't want to make small talk?"

Nico shrugged. "I've been here since seven."

Yes, Igor made sure when Vaslav said *now*, he meant not one second later this time around. But that didn't mean he had to actually grace Nico with his presence or attention until he wanted to. So, the man had sat just outside the gates of the estate, where the neighbors across the large road on their own private property would be able to see him should they look out the window.

Maybe not *who* unless they had a pair of binoculars, but that wasn't the point. He only wanted Nico to wait.

Anyone who believed Vaslav had a heart left would probably think those hours Nico sat in his car were meant to give him time to find another way out of the situation they found themselves in. Except that just wasn't the case. It was only their easy friendship over the years and shared memories that even allowed Nico to sit in the place he did beside Vaslav.

That was *a lot*.

Vaslav demanded far more than just friendship and a past when it came to forgiving those who he had extended his trust after they broke it in some way. When he said he didn't trust anybody, he meant that. Loyalty was one thing, and obviously a required trait in the handful of people he kept around him, but that trust?

Priceless to a man like him, and once gone, there was no going back.

He didn't so much as break bonds between himself and those he felt betrayed him as much as he just obliterated them. All at once. No questions asked. There was not a soul on earth who could unring that bell for Vaslav once it was rung.

That was his entire life in a nutshell.

Behind him laid a road he'd paved of broken bodies, burned bridges, and ruined lives from doing this very thing time and time again. Some, like his mother, were not the same because from practically the start, well, he'd known not to trust the bitch.

Others, though, like Nico …

Vaslav never said his choices didn't hurt.

That didn't mean they were *wrong*.

Nothing he did was ever wrong.

"Do you remember the first night we met?" Vaslav asked.

He'd seated himself in the chair opposite of his friend, letting his axe rest against his leg while he folded his other ankle over the same knee.

Finally, he earned a reaction from Nico when the man smiled a bit as he bobbed his head. "You were a very different man then."

"Or it was just a different time, yes?"

A decade and a half ago, he'd been protecting the Russian oligarchs and still trying to find his footing in the brotherhood outside of prison walls. Just because he had been given his eight-pointed stars on his shoulders in prison, and earned spires on his chest for his time, meant nothing in the world of the wealthy and elite outside of cement and bars.

Mostly.

It counted a little for respect.

Maybe he'd been a bit lucky in the fact that his last name came with a bit of power and privilege— sometimes, that was the only thing to get him through the front door with some of the men who shook his hand over the years.

"The political ball, wasn't it?" Nico asked.

"The same night I meant Abram and Irina."

A short, hard breath split from Nico's lips, and he dropped Vaslav's gaze. His friend didn't need him to fill in that gap—how could either of them forget the night that would change the course of their history forever?

Not just him and Nico, but Irina and her father.

All of them changed after that.

Nico, then only thirty-four while Vaslav had just passed his thirtieth, was the bull tasked with personally guarding and minding the only daughter of Russia's most notorious crime boss. Back then, there wasn't a substance, gun, or pussy bought in the country that wasn't owned or touched in some way by Abram Federov's brigadiers. He even extended his control and territory into Europe, and in Canada and the states through smaller factions that had set up shop and grew over time.

The man was untouchable.

To sit at his table was a deal with the devil, and a person didn't even need to know they'd handed over their soul before Abram had already taken it.

"She wore white that night," Nico said.

Vas nodded, rocking a bit in the chair from the action. "All silk and chiffon. I have pictures."

And sky-high heels.

When a man was six-foot-eight inches tall, it was hard to miss a woman who would almost meet him eye-for-eye in a pair of six-inch stilettos.

Vaslav blinked, then, into the growing darkness of the property, and his memories flashing in the back of his mind. What ones remained, anyway. He could still see Irina's eyes from that night—maybe he'd mapped them in seconds and imprinted them to his memory forever. It was the first thing he'd noticed about her, and one of the few things his memory allowed him to keep.

Later, she told him, "*All I saw was your smile.*"

He'd loved her dark, dry humor the most. And how she'd never hidden anything from him until the very end.

By then, it was already too late.

"You were gone there for a second," Nico noted, his murmur reaching through the haze of Vaslav's past flashing in front of his eyes to rip him right out of it in a second flat.

"Did Khristina enjoy the trip, at least?"

Nico's brow dropped at the sudden change in topic; just like before, he slumped back into the chair making Vaslav even more aware of how rumpled the man's clothes seemed. "Of course, she did. She's twenty-one, never been to Barbados, and had me eating out of the palm of her hand for days. It was everything I promised her it would be."

"She was happy, you mean."

Another sigh left his friend. Nico's standard black-on-black-on-black three-piece suit, including shined, Italian leather loafers, just didn't have the same sharpness it usually did. Those bags under his old friend's eyes didn't help, either, considering how deep they made his crows feet appear.

He'd turned fifty on that island with his new, very young bride, and had he just stayed in Russia after Vaslav found out the loan he'd given Feliks ... had he not run, in a way, he might have been forgiven.

Or at least, forgotten.

It couldn't work that way, now.

"They say fifty hits you hard," Vaslav said, scrubbing his hand down his jaw while he stared up at the dark clouds rolling through the blackening sky. Might it rain? "You didn't really run, did you? You just didn't want to disappoint Khristina."

"She told me yesterday that she's pregnant."

"They'll be taken care of," Vaslav assured instantly, wanting that clear between them.

And they would, no matter what happened tonight. It was a promise he kept because despite the men who believed women and children had no place in their world, Vaslav found—often—those same women and children were simply victims of circumstance and love. Rarely did people choose who they loved. Instead, love made the choice for them.

A man's sins should be his own.

"I'll make sure of it," he added.

Nico pulled in a shaky breath, then, and once more, couldn't meet the eyes of the man who had called him there in the first place. "Will they?"

"You could have chosen not to come tonight. Why question me when you did? You had to know."

"*Fuck*—how long before you found me, huh? How much worse does it get, then?"

"I trusted you, Nico."

"I know," his friend rushed to say, every word strained. "And no explanation is going to make it better because I fucked up, Vas. I don't even have an excuse. I promise it wasn't our money—*your* money, though. It never moved through any hand that touches yours before it went to his."

"Doesn't matter. I made the call—he was already *dead*."

Even walking with a heart still beating, the second

that Vaslav killed Feliks' father, took over the organization, and all but shit on the Abramov name and legacy, the man was an untouchable. And not in a good way. Any business with Feliks would be seen as a stain. Trash was still trash no matter where it landed.

"It's been six damn years, Vas!" Nico hissed.

"You don't get to decide when this ends for him. If I wanted that bastard to walk the streets of Moscow for another ten years as a fucking pariah before I put him out of his misery, that was *my* right to do so. Maybe it was your money to give, but you clearly didn't consider that cost would be far higher than you were willing to pay, comrade."

Tipping his chin up and Vaslav stood from the chair, Nico stared hard at him. There were so many things the two of them could have said—better memories to relive, almost a lifetime to go through together, if they wanted.

That was all over, though.

Vaslav didn't like to go back with people who weren't taking him forward.

"Do you want to know why?" Nico asked.

"Would it matter?"

"No, Vas. It won't."

"There's your answer."

"They all said you wouldn't do it," Nico uttered.

Yeah, he bet. Igor when he called to demand his presence. Maybe even Nico's wife, if she knew *anything* about his dealings. Definitely Natalia on her way out of the estate. Everyone of them probably told Nico the same thing.

He won't kill you, you're his best friend.

The world around him kept expecting a beast to

suddenly grow into a man.

"I wanted to believe you wouldn't do it, Vas."

"Well, don't expect me to apologize."

Nico had been too busy keeping his gaze locked on Vaslav that he didn't even notice the man had picked up his axe when he stood. His final words to Nico were punctuated with the weapon swinging over his shoulder, so he could catch the handle fast with both hands to swing it forward.

He'd moved the coffee table earlier, and even rearranged the chairs.

Nico didn't even have time to sit straight in his chair before the axe came down, crushing his face with a morbid crunch and one last squeak. There wasn't even a scream. Vaslav had two things to his favor—a mighty swing, and one hell of an aim.

Practice made perfect.

Every single time.

*

Igor found Vaslav still sitting in the rattan chair—but with a lit cigarette dangling from his lips—as the rain began to drizzle. At least, the summer rain was warm. His head of security didn't make it halfway down the path before his walk came to a complete stop, and he cursed under his breath.

Nico's head flopped back on the chair across from Vaslav still had the axe embedded into his face. Well, the blood had stopped flowing now, but there was quite a significant puddle down the man's body and under him on the grass.

The chair was ruined.

"I needed a new set anyway," he told Igor.

"You really fucking did it."

Vaslav only sighed.

It took Igor several more minutes before he joined Vaslav at the seating area in front of the fire pit. He opted for the loveseat, his gaze darting between his boss and the body that he would soon have to deal with.

Everybody needed a moment when it came to death. He allowed Igor to take his, after all, he'd worked alongside Nico for the last six years after Vaslav had taken over as boss.

"Do you know why I liked you—why I put you where I did?"

Igor glanced his way. A million questions raced in his dark gaze, but Vaslav had no intention of answering any of them. "What?"

"I met you when you were barely thirty-two, but you took orders well and were no-nonsense about it."

"Not much has changed, has it?"

Vaslav tipped his head toward Nico's corpse, uttering, "I don't know, but I'm hoping that after tonight, I'll have to speak less than twice."

Igor swallowed hard.

Good.

Another point made.

Standing from the chair, Vaslav finished the one cigarette he'd pilfered from Mira's purse earlier. She wouldn't even notice it missing, and he couldn't afford more nicotine lest it flare yet another migraine to put him out of commission for days.

"You know he only did it—gave Feliks money, I mean—because the asshole told him Irina wouldn't have wanted to see the place fall like it was."

Vaslav took another breath in, and then took his

time letting it out. It seemed Nico had been right, then. It didn't matter his reason why; Vaslav still would have swung that axe had he known.

"Igor," Vaslav murmured.

It was the shift of the man's clothes that told Vaslav he had turned to look at him.

"Someday, you're going to be the one making these kinds of choices. Don't for one second think it's easy."

It took the younger man a second to absorb the quiet statement. He still didn't seem to have a firm grasp on what Vaslav meant when Igor said, "Some people might call me a monster, Vas, but that doesn't mean I want to do monstrous things because of it, too."

Well, that was part of the problem.

"Monsters aren't born, comrade." *Look at me.* "They're made."

Not waiting for a further reply, Vaslav headed for the cobblestone path, leaving his mess behind. Over his shoulder, he told his only living friend, "Keep my axe."

"And the garbage bags are in the shed," Igor deadpanned. "I know."

"You think you'd be happy."

"For what?"

"I can still swing the damn thing."

"*So?*" Igor asked, frustration rising like his tone.

Vaslav chuckled, continuing his trek to the back of the house. "Every other day of the week, on the other hand, you think I'm dying."

Silence answered that.

What more really needed to be said?

9.

For the second time in less than two weeks, Vera opened the front door of her home to find a potted plant sitting on the stoop. In a square, simple terracotta pot, the green branches that stuck up from dark soil made her pause. With the phone already in her hand, she considered calling her mother right back to pass her thanks along to her father.

Something about the plant stopped her, though.

Vera even tilted her head to the side a bit, already curious. She expected to bend down and flip the plain white tag over to find something from the greenhouse where it had been sold, but the handwriting spelling out instructions for planting and caring for the Syringa vulgaris accompanied no other information.

Krasavitsa Moskvy someone had written in English under the name of the plant. Though she already knew what that meant, the writing continued to say *Beauty of Moscow. Plant next spring, water well once a week until then, and keep it in the sun as much as you can. A thank you. - V*

Vera surveyed the quiet stoop and street for any sign of the person who had left the lilac shrub, but she found no one. Who knew when they had left it? She really should put that camera on her front door like her father had suggested more than a few times already.

The bright, early August sun overhead beamed down on Vera and the pot in her hands as she straightened up with it to give the shrub a closer look.

"He didn't stay very long," called her neighbor from his yard.

"Who?"

The man pointed at the pot. "Whoever dropped off that. Didn't take his sunglasses off, didn't say hi when he walked past, and the guy waiting on the street already had his door open again before he got back. I'm surprised you didn't hear the tires squealing."

Vera peered at the cursive *V* on the white card stock with the instructions. The jagged hole through the thick paper and twine used to lop through it to tie the card to a branch seemed hasty while the handwritten note had clearly taken more than a minute.

"Did you find yourself an admirer, Vera?" her neighbor asked.

She gave the man a look. "Did you sneak up my steps and read what was on this?"

She wasn't offended. Anatoly was a good neighbor in the way he kept an eye out for anything his fellow neighbors might need to watch out for. The retired doctor's only real companions since his wife died was his community.

Vera didn't mind his nosiness.

"Maybe," her neighbor said, chuckling. "You didn't answer my question, either young lady."

Vera glanced down at the note again, parroting his smartass reply right back, *"Maybe."*

Her teasing was just that, though. A joke. Her father was the only man who had someone leave flowers or plants for her to love and nurture, seeing as he knew about her hobby that she'd picked up after quitting ballet full time. What else was she going to spend her time doing?

Otherwise, the standard birthday flowers or other important events came with bouquets, but not random lilac shrubs in a terracotta pot that looked as though it had seen a few plants before the one that now called it home.

And that made her just a little more than curious about it. Too bad she didn't have the time to consider it.

"How much longer are you going to stare at that before you take it in the house?"

"Mind your business, Mr. Anatoly. And hey, we're supposed to get rain tomorrow," she told her neighbor. "Stop wasting water."

The old man laughed, even daring to lift his garden hose higher to send a spray of cold water dangerously close to her villa stoop. The threat of getting wet, but also not wanting to be late for her ballet class, sent Vera back inside with a new plant to add to her collection. She would have to come back to the plant, and the stranger who'd left it behind, later.

But even as she exited the villa again, locked the door, and shared lighthearted jabs with her neighbor along the fence line of their properties, the surprise gift wasn't far from her mind.

Who left it?

And what had he been thanking her for?

*

Vera tried to be as understanding and open as she could while one of her only male pupils, twelve-year-old Ivan, closed himself off entirely from her. Folding his arms over his chest, the young man sunk his back harder against the wall of the darkened studio and pulled one foot up on the bench he sat on. It was the way he'd set his lips in a firm line while he refused to meet her gaze even after she asked him to that said more than he was willing to.

The boy didn't want to hear her.

He'd already made up his mind.

Vera still couldn't help but try ...

Despite knowing she wasn't supposed to remain at the studio any longer than necessary after she'd finished teaching her free class for The Swan House, Vera hadn't been able to say no when Ivan asked if they could chat when all the kids had filtered out. Out of all the kids, she had a handful that she considered high risk for different reasons. Often, the ballet classes were their only extra curricular activity. They were kids with maybe one parent, like Ivan who lived with his single-mom that worked forty-five-plus-hour work weeks just to pay their rent and keep them fed. Kids that just needed a little extra attention or simply someone to talk to when they were having a bad day.

Ivan was one of those kids.

"You're sure you want to quit?" she asked Ivan once more. "At least, be sure it's the choice you want to make. And if it is, then look me in my face and say so."

The twelve-year-old wouldn't do it.

No matter how long Vera remained kneeling in front of him, *willing* the kid silently to even try. Instead, he let out an annoyed sigh.

"I don't think it's because you don't have time like you told me," Vera told him, deciding to just get right to the point. "I think it has something to do with that group of boys you've been hanging out with for the last month or so. Sometimes they come with you and hang out across the street while you're in here?"

One could lead a horse directly to water, but they couldn't make it drink. The same could be said for an almost-teenage-boy with a group of friends who determined what was cool. She had a feeling those boys could find a million other things to do to waste their time, and ballet probably wasn't one of them.

"Maybe I want to play soccer," Ivan said suddenly.

"Then, maybe you should. And you've also been doing ballet with me since you were eight, I know you love it—you've said so—so why do you want to quit?"

He hadn't been expecting her fast question if the dip of his eyebrows was any indication. Not that it really prompted the kid to come back with a reply because instead, he just shut down and off again with his arms over his chest and his back to the wall.

"Ivan," Vera tried to say.

The boy shrugged one shoulder jerkily. "I already told my mom, too. I'm quitting. That's it."

"But you still came for one last class, huh?" Vera stood up, eyeing the boy's sweatpants he had started to wear to class for the last couple weeks. That was her first hint one of his friends, or the entire group, had started to make comments.

Why were kids mean sometimes?

Couldn't people just let people be?

Who cared if a boy wanted to dance—if he found peace wearing tights and flying across a stage—what would it hurt if he was great at it and loved it?

Why couldn't he just *be*?

"You know," Vera told Ivan as he stood from the bench and gathered his gym bag from the floor between them, "it's okay to like something that someone else doesn't like, Ivan. The older you get, the less you'll care what others think about you. You'll notice that people won't have much to say then about what you do because they've finally figured out it's better to just worry about themselves."

The boy heaved the bag over his shoulder. "Yeah, well …"

Not right now, she could hear practically him saying in his head with a roll of his eyes.

"You can come back anytime."

Ivan met her gaze, then. "Yeah?"

Vera nodded. "I'll keep your name on the list for the rest of the year. Just in case you do want to come back, okay?"

"I probably won't, though."

Those quiet words hurt her.

Vera didn't say so. "And that's okay, too. As long as you're happy, Ivan."

"Thanks, Miss Vera."

She remained kneeling on the floor as Ivan headed out of the studio, the squeak of his sneakers on the hardwood floor echoing long after the kid was gone. The kids couldn't possibly know it, but she needed them as much as they sometimes needed her. Or even more, really. She invested so much time, energy and love to them and their classes; in a way, it was the only thing she had left of what used to be her life.

That change had come so abruptly back then; it altogether knocked her off her feet, and instantly destroyed what was supposed to be her future. Having the chance to teach the kids ballet had felt like a saving grace at the time.

She'd never considered this might end someday, too.

What happened then?

What would she do then?

Vera couldn't say how many minutes passed with her frozen on the studio floor, lost to the grief caused by her constant state of limbo, but it had to be more time than Feliks considered acceptable. His personal assistant's voice echoed over the large, dark space, yanking Vera from her private disgrace.

"Can you hear me, or what?"

The assistant was a constant fixture in Feliks' orbit although the woman didn't know a damn thing about the world of ballet. Actually, Vera wasn't even sure if Nadya could dance considering the stick of ice that must have been stuck up her ass.

She was that type.

It always rubbed Vera wrong.

"*Yes*, I hear you," Vera snapped back, not bothering to turn and face Nadya while her face was still wet with tears. "Tell Feliks I'm going."

"I said, he wants to see you in his office, actually. So, you didn't hear me."

Vera couldn't even laugh or refuse the rude woman—by the time she'd wiped her face and stood from the floor, Nadya had vanished from the studio. Left alone, too angry for her own good, and more annoyed than ever with Feliks, she could only ask, "What now?"

10.

"What is your damn problem?"

Feliks probably hadn't expected Vera to storm into his office without even knocking first, but he barely showed a hint of surprise.

"Take your pick," the man replied, sounding bored. "I have an entire list, actually."

"That would concern me?"

At that, Feliks didn't respond.

She was more shocked to see the space empty of people except for him, standing in his staple black suit where he leaned against the corner of the ornate black desk.

There was always *someone* in here with him. He used the space to entertain more often than work. Every piece of furniture, art, or otherwise was placed as a conversation piece to brag about or show of some sort of wealth or skill.

It wasn't normal, and she instantly went on guard.

"You've been incredibly—*graciously*—beneficial to

The Swan House, and that's where my respect for you came from, Vera. You understand that, yes?"

Her loose stance stiffened a bit at his remarks. Of course, she knew her presence even after her accident here had been important for the company's image and reputation. He said it was beneficial like that meant more than Vera was aware.

"I only wanted to be here," she replied. "The details never really mattered to me, Feliks."

He nodded, a hint of a smile curving the edge of his mouth, but he didn't quite let it bloom before raising his head and meeting her gaze. She didn't find contempt staring back in his dark eyes—just a resignation.

A heaviness.

She seemed to recognize that look in others, now, even when she wasn't trying to find it. Like her soul could feel the weight life had left on other people's shoulders.

It was unfortunate that being someone who was empathetic to others often left her learning the harshest of lessons. She trusted too easily—even the man standing in front of her had once been proof of that.

"You weren't even the tenth ballerina I had fucked," he noted.

The crassness of his statement had Vera standing ramrod straight. "Excuse me?"

Yes, she knew that. He was only pouring salt in the wound when he pointed it out, though. Some things were better left unsaid.

"Go to hell, Feliks," Vera said, spinning on her heels to leave. "I'm done. With you and with this whole place."

She planned to leave that room—and the building—with the same furious speed she'd entered it. But this time, she wouldn't be coming back.

Vera didn't *have* to take this man's abuse; in whatever form it came her way. His total disregard for her had started the second she left his ass, and she only put up with it for this long because The Swan House continued to call her home. She wouldn't stay there and keep doing it, however.

His voice calling after her stopped Vera in the office's doorway when he said, "You were the only one I respected enough not to chase you out of my sight once I'd had enough of you, though."

She spun right back around, not giving a single damn how crazy she probably looked when she pointed a finger at him and shouted, "You didn't throw me away, asshole! I was done with *you*! And don't forget it this time, either."

"You're right." The fight didn't leave Vera at his admission, but Feliks also wasn't done yet. "Seems like you're still missing the point, no? Despite not really caring about a piece of ass that continued to taunt me in these halls, I gave you as much as you reasonably wanted because it was beneficial for me to do so."

Oh, really?

"Not anymore," she said, turning to leave.

"Not for a long time, Vera, that's the sad truth," Feliks hollered after her as she headed into the large hall. "I tried to warn you, didn't I? To mind your business? Why couldn't you just do that?"

She didn't care to ask him what he meant.

Vera kept walking.

"You have a contract, Vera!"

She scoffed. "That expired last month—check the dates!"

In fact, she'd known that they had let her standard contract—that guaranteed the free classes complete funding and control to her in exchange for her time and a certain number of charity events a year—expire. Vera purposely made the choice to say nothing about it or bring it up until she had worked through some of her recent feelings regarding The Swan House and her purpose for being there.

Apparently, that was the right thing to do. Again, her gut *never* led her wrong.

By the time she reached the end of the hallway where the stairwell was, Feliks had come to stand in front of his office doorway. She took one second to stop at the top of the stairs, glancing over her shoulder to glare at the man who hadn't even taken the time to explain why he wanted her in his office in the first place.

"You're really going to do this to those kids?" he asked, his words traveling down the corridor of ballerina portraits.

So cruelly, it stung.

Because she couldn't even deny it—he was right. Truth be told, she was the only person who could maintain the classes and schedule the way she did given the staff and dancers for the company were down to a fraction of what they had once been. There was nobody else to continue what she had started. It would end all at once for those kids.

She could already see their heartbroken little faces.

"I did try to warn you," Feliks said again. "I'll see you in the studio on Monday, Vera! Whether it's to tell those kids you're done with this place, or not."

Then, he stepped back inside his office.

Vera heard the doors slam shut, but she was already racing down the stairs, hating him for calling her on her bluff like that. He'd tried to warn her—but about *what?*

That question chased her to the ground level of The Swan House, and down another corridor that led to the grand entrance. It was the tears she didn't bother to hide, though. Every single person she passed watched her cry.

It hurt to leave her world behind, but she was done pretending like this place still felt like home.

It didn't.

*

Vera was just around the corner from her villa when she realized how far she'd walked while still lost in her thoughts. Almost mechanically, or robotically, without even thinking about it. She hadn't even taken the time to consider her surroundings, and as her street came into view, her tears had long since dried.

She could have called a cab and made it home in mere minutes, but the walk helped to clear her mind. At least enough to think about … well, about what was next. Or what she should do next. Even the tiniest shred of her dignity in Feliks' hand could be a dangerous thing. If she went back to The Swan House on Monday, and it wasn't to explain to the kids she was quitting … then Feliks' was already winning. He would use this in some way whether to manipulate her in some way in the future, or even if it was just to hurt her pride. Either way, his sick sense of satisfaction would be the same.

But the kids, she told herself.

And yourself, Vera could almost hear her father telling her. All her life, he demanded she think of herself. She almost hadn't existed, after all, nearly killed alongside her biological mother while Gia was in her final few weeks of pregnancy. He'd wanted her to live, told her she could do anything, and he'd make it happen as long as she wanted it.

If only things were simple.

She could quit, like she wanted and knew she should, but what good did that do for anyone? The kids would lose a valuable program, and Vera would be back to square one. Like the day she woke up after her surgery, staring straight at her elevated, heavily bandaged ankle and foot, and not knowing anything about what would happen next.

Maybe that was what held Vera back the most. Or rather, it was her greatest fear. Nothing else scared her quite the same. She'd already been a failure, after all. Even if it was by the mistake of others; it didn't matter. She'd failed entirely at the height of her career and survived that shame.

It was always the *what now* that left her terrified. The unknown future ahead of her, days she saw filled with nothingness because she had nothing else except ballet.

Who cared if she had money? What did it matter if she never needed to find a job, have another career, or even lift a finger for the rest of her life?

None of that meant anything to Vera when all she could see was nothing waiting in front of her. No goal to achieve. No dreams to chase. Was that even a real life to live?

Was this what it meant to be *lost*?

"Miss Avdonin—*Vera* Avdonin, yes?"

Still distracted by her inner turmoil, Vera had managed to walk almost to her drive without noticing. She couldn't miss the towering bull of a man standing in the middle of the sidewalk right in front of her villa as soon as her head popped up, though. Or the black SUV parked directly in front of her villa.

"Sorry, did you not hear me?" the stranger asked.

"I didn't. Who are you?"

He smiled, and it was the easiness of it that gave his face a friendly quality. At the sight of it, she could almost forget that she couldn't pass him because he took up most of the sidewalk with his feet planted shoulder-width apart and arms folded over his broad chest.

"Friends call me Igor," he told her. "I wasn't sure whether you'd prefer the ballet house or yours for this, so I hope you don't mind."

She wasn't entirely concerned about the man considering the sun hadn't even set, and a family who lived in a villa further down were walking their Huskies.

"What is *this*, exactly?" Vera asked back, waving a hand between them.

He chuckled and removed the aviator sunglasses that had been hiding a good portion of his upper face. His brown gaze landed on her, and she recognized him in an instant.

"You're the guy that helped Feliks that day in the gallery," Vera said. "The man who fell, is he okay?"

Weeks and weeks had passed since that event, but not one day went by that she didn't wonder about the man. For the obvious reasons, but also because after the way Feliks had behaved during lunch, she wondered who the mysterious man was.

Igor waved his hand, still holding the sunglasses. "That's me. As for your other question …" His laugh came out a little dry. "That just depends."

On what? Because she thought her question and the incident in question were straightforward.

Vera chose not to point that out because his sunglasses had reminded her of something else. Or rather, something that someone else had said to her. Mr. Anatoly, her neighbor. His description of the man and vehicle possibly matched Igor and his SUV, except one person was missing.

"Did he leave me a shrub as a thank you?" she asked.

Igor shrugged as he put his sunglasses back on. "His name is Vaslav, and he'd like to invite you for tea."

Vaslav.

For a second, Vera wasn't quite sure what to say. As fast as she connected that dot, another started to take form in her mind. Was that what Feliks had meant—about warning her?

She didn't exactly feel scared, but that didn't stop Vera's gaze from drifting over the visible tattoos on Igor's hands. Mostly importantly, the distinctive upturned spider on the back of his left one.

Vera had just enough of an understanding about men who joined the traditional brotherhood to recognize a tattoo like that. She'd been so concerned with *Vaslav* that day on the floor that she had barely noticed his visible tattoos at the time. But when she'd had the chance to return to her memories, she could remember she'd had seen some, too.

Just not *what*, specifically.

The same, maybe?

"Tea?" she asked.

"Tea," Igor responded.

"First, a question," Vera returned. "Do you know who I—"

"I know a great deal about you. Likely more than you would be comfortable with knowing that I know, really. That's the nature of my job for a particularly important man. Do you understand?"

She glanced at his tattooed hands, and that time, Igor didn't miss it. "Important, or dangerous?"

"It can be both."

"Everything okay, Vera?"

The call from her right drew Vera's attention to the man who had come out to stand on the front stoop of his villa beside hers. Mr. Anatoly probably couldn't do much at his age, but one wouldn't think so as much by the glower he leveled on Igor in that moment.

"Back again—where's your friend, the one you were driving around?" the old, retired doctor asked Igor directly.

As she suspected, nothing went unnoticed in her neighborhood.

"He *would* notice me if I went missing," Vera joked quietly to Igor, knowing her neighbor couldn't hear.

Well, partly joking.

The warning still applied.

"Point taken," Igor replied without missing a beat, "but it is just tea."

"With a dangerous man, you said."

"Apparently, *you've* been worried about him." He flipped his hands up as if to silently say *no offense.* "You did ask about him, I'm only saying."

"Hey. He brought me a shrub, first!"

And now Vera had to wonder ... "Did he do that because you looked into me—because you found out I liked plants because I often have them sent to my address?"

Igor didn't reply to that.

Vera figured that was her answer.

Who was this *Vaslav*?

And why was he looking into her in the first place?

"I was only there to see him fall," she said, more to herself than the man in front of her on the sidewalk. "I just tried to help, and he's looking into my interests and hobbies?"

It might be a little concerning if she wasn't so ... curious.

That probably wasn't a good thing.

Igor scratched at the side of his neck, muttering, "The man's about half insane, and if not, there's a good damn chance Vaslav Pashkov has already lost his mind, and he's gotten really good at hiding it. I've learned over the years not to ask a question more than once, and you don't get many answers about a person that way, you see. If you expect me to know why he looked into you, the answer is yes, because you saw him fall and tried to help. That is what I know."

She appreciated his bluntness.

"Vera?" Mr. Anatoly called again.

"Everything's fine," she told her neighbor.

"You're sure?"

"*Da.*"

She had to repeat it one more time before Mr. Anatoly finally headed back inside his villa. She bet he watched her from the shaded windows framing his entrance, though.

"Who is he?" she asked Igor.

That was the real question.

The *important* one, likely.

"I can't tell you that, nobody could," Igor replied. "But this evening, he's just a man in a large house, practically alone, who would like to have tea with a woman who showed him kindness. Or that was what he barked at me when I asked. I am not in the business of asking my boss to repeat himself, frankly."

Vera eyed her own villa, and even thought about the phone in her hand. "Is it stupid that I'm actually considering saying yes?"

"I'm not here to offer a personal opinion about with whom you spend your time, although if it counts, I can't say Vas means you any harm."

Now he was *Vas*?

Vera shifted the messenger bag hanging off her shoulder to relieve a bit of the weight, deciding her choice as fast as it took to give Igor a nod. "Lucky for him, I have nothing better to do at the moment."

And she really did want to find out if he was okay.

Igor was already reaching for the rear passenger door of his SUV. "I'll drive."

She liked his dry humor already.

11.

"*You've arrived at—*"

"See, I didn't lie about the address," Igor boomed over the feminine, but still robotic, voice of the stereo's GPS system.

Vera rolled her eyes in response, but still saved a drafted text that she had typed out just in case. It had taken her twice as long to type the three-word text to her father; the address in both Russian and English because she was sure he would want both. She would only send it if she needed to, but so far, nothing seemed amiss.

Igor kept her laughing on the drive.

In his own special way.

In the backseat, Vera's gaze turned away from the gated-driveway Igor had parked in. It didn't matter because she could still see the view of the three-level Federal Colonial up the long drive where the landscape inclined just enough to make the house appear like it waited on the top of a hill. The cracked, but paved, driveway winded right, and then left. But it was what hugged the driveway on either side just beyond the gate that made Vera smile.

Even though they weren't in bloom, she recognized the two adult lilac trees by their shape and greenery.

"You're lucky, no?" Igor asked her.

"Why's that?"

Igor replied as he opened his door and jumped out. "Most guests have to walk from here."

"He makes people walk four hundred feet just to visit him?"

"Exactly. And he wonders why people *don't.*"

He didn't give her the chance to respond before he slammed the door shut, his laughter muffled through the glass Vera watched him head for the gate and admired the way ivy covered almost the entirety of the gray brick on the front of the massive home at the same time.

It didn't take Igor long at all to unlock the old iron gate and swing both arms wide open beyond the stone pillars holding them up. He had jumped back in the SUV, and the vehicle lurched forward before he had even shut the driver's door again.

"There's only one rule today," Igor said, glancing at her in the rearview mirror as they crawled up the small hill, closer to the house.

"What's that?"

"No phones in the house."

Vera met his stare, then. "That hardly seems—"

"It's non-negotiable, sweetheart. He wouldn't care if you were his mother yeah, no phones in the fucking house."

The hill flattened at the top where the driveway widened into a massive block that covered most of the front of the house. Igor parked next to the towering circle of birch trees in the very middle, likely the only shade for the front of the house when the sun was high in the sky. She was entirely unsurprised to see terracotta pots lining the entire front of the house, and even the steps of the wide stone staircase leading up to the double front doors. She bet every little shrub in each of those pots matched the one she had at her villa.

"Phone?"

Igor's sudden demand brought Vera back to the present. Her admiration of the home and property was gone in an instant as Igor's hand popped palm up between the front seats, not giving her any time to really think.

"Now, come on," he said.

Dammit.

She should have sent that text to her father when she had the chance … but why worry Demyan, who was all the way across the world, and not actually capable of helping her, should she need it?

Besides, she'd never asked him for permission to do something before. Not since she turned eighteen, anyway.

Vera slapped her phone into Igor's palm.

"*Spasibo*," the man thanked her. "Out you go—now you're on your own."

"Seriously?"

Igor shrugged, and flopped back into his seat. "I did my required time with Vaslav today, thank you."

"You make him sound like—"

"A beast," the man interjected. "He's a beast on his best days. And don't you forget it."

*

Vera thought she should be more nervous as she climbed the fifteen stairs—she counted each one—that led up to the entrance of the house. The double doors were older than they first appeared because once she stood on the circular woven mat in front of them, she could see where the brown paint had started to crack and peel along the hinges and brass knocker. The only thing that looked new or modern on the door was the curved handle with a latch and the three deadbolts in a line above.

"Mind Marrow, if you see him," he called behind her.

Vera glanced back at Igor who had come to stand at the front of the SUV where she could see him around the line of birch trees.

"What?"

"Marrow—the water dog. He's a bit wilder than his master. Sometimes, we don't see him for weeks."

"How do I *mind* him?" she asked.

"By keeping a distance."

Great.

She didn't even know what a *water dog* looked like.

A creak sent Vera spinning back around. The short woman with blonde and gray-streaked hair pulled into a tight bun wasn't what she expected to see.

"*Zdravstvuyte, miss,*" the woman greeted. Her flat gray dress and the fact she wouldn't meet Vera's gaze, staring instead directly at her mouth, took her aback. If she noticed, the woman didn't show it when she said, "I'm Mira. Mr. Pashkov is in the back. I'll take you that way."

She bet guests weren't welcomed to wander, either.

Mira barely gave Vera time to learn her name properly before she had spun around to open the heavy, thick oak door wider. Slate gray tile welcomed the guests into a grand entrance complete with an hourglass shaped stairwell leading up to the south or east side of the upper levels. A second, smaller matching staircase continued above the glittering ropes of crystals hanging down from a massive chandelier to what must have been the third level.

She had been inside beautiful homes before. Danced in palaces, too. Even her own parents own a mansion in the gated suburbs of New York that their wealthy neighbors envied.

But as she walked over the worn black rug that started on the tile and crawled up the staircase, Vera thought there was something unique about this place. Not that she could quite put her finger on it, but it may have been the walls upon walls of history.

Of Moscow. A family. Photographs that spanned generations with just a quick look. There were even paintings hung high that she dared to say were too old to even dust—maybe only the frames. She mostly followed the sound of Mira's footsteps leading her across the entrance as she tried to take in every high wall in the entrance, filled with … too much.

Then, the woman cleared her throat. "Right down at the end."

Vera wasn't even embarrassed to be caught gawking at what could be considered a museum of images—but of what?

"Thanks," she replied.

Mira dipped a bit her way, almost a bow but not quite. "Miss. *Net, spasibo.*"

She said nothing else before disappearing around

the staircase, and Vera listened to the patter of Mira's footsteps all the way to the very top.

The dark wood-paneled corridor leading into the back of the house waited for her once she was alone. On one side, she could see light spilling into the shadowed space. On the other, matching twin doors were closed tight.

She headed that way.

Once she stood in between the two, her stranger had already laid eyes on her.

"Do you have a place to plant the shrub?" he asked in Russian.

"Vaslav Pashkov?"

Standing behind his desk, he was visible from Vera's position in the hall. Anyone walking into the man's office would see him there, whether sitting or standing, and would probably be shocked at the side of the man against the big desk. It should have been the centerpiece.

She found he still kind of dominated the space and room.

Unlike Igor, Vaslav didn't have the pounds of large muscle making his already tall frame imposing. Instead, he was just *tall*, his chest broad under his silk dress shirt, and the fabric was tight around strong arms.

"I'm sorry—did you want to do an introduction?" he asked her.

Vera shrugged, and stepped forward into the room to see the large TV on one wall, the rows of bookshelves and even the sitting area in front of the windows that already had tea waiting on the coffee table's glass top.

"I only just learned your name today, and you

could at least pretend like you don't know mine," she explained. "I couldn't forget your face, but I didn't know—"

"It scared you," he said, frankly. "My ... spell."

"Is that what you call it?"

That seemed like a medical event to her that would be important to understand. Especially if it was part of a larger picture.

Vaslav waved one hand, as if silently saying *oh, well* before dropping ungraciously into his chair. He dragged a hand through his black hair, his studious blue gaze still locked onto her. Vera didn't think she was very much to look at, walking into that room— *compared* to the room. She still had on the leggings she had opted to wear over her leotard for class, and a white pair of sneakers that matched the color of her loose, cashmere shawl. He still took his time giving her a good once over.

"What, there weren't enough pictures of me in all the information you gathered?"

At that question, Vaslav's gaze lifted to slam into hers. "Actually, no. Not a lot of recent ones. I see Igor still needs his tongue pickled."

Damn.

She appreciated his honesty, but Vera still blinked a bit at the dip in his tone. She'd almost call it murderous if his expression had changed to match. But it didn't. "He's funny, really. I like him."

The man lifted one thick, dark eyebrow and for a second, she was lost in the lines of his face. Vera liked older men. She wasn't a liar, so if she was asked where that preference of hers began, she would say it was from the start. Always had, although more than once, it had placed her amid people who had more life

experience than her. She sought that out in people—
in *men*. Their experience and stability. She wanted to
feel a certain way in the arms of a man, and those her
age typically didn't invoke what she was looking for.

She hadn't expected to find that sense of
domineering, possessiveness standing in the den of a
stranger. Even if he was a handsome one. It took
Vera off guard.

"Are you okay?" she asked him.

Vaslav chuckled. "Better than I was that day in the
gallery."

"Hmm."

"Not what you were looking for?"

"Well, I did get to ask you—that's more than I
knew before," she returned easily.

Vaslav was a beautiful man, but she wondered if
people could handle the intensity of his stare long
enough to notice. Or did the scar that marred the
right side of his face only add to the man's severity?

His angular jaw and a strong chin hardened his
feature, making that scar more noticeable in the way it
twisted and pulled with his expressions. All the same,
she could appreciate the way his wider nose fit the
rest of his chiseled profile, and despite the way his
gaze squinted a bit in his stare, like one would in
anger, he still smiled.

Or rather, she saw a hint of one.

"I'm sorry," Vera said.

Vaslav stood up from his chair, working on rolling
up one white silk sleeve before moving onto the
other. "For what? Tea?"

Vera nodded. "I have time for a cup."

"And the apology?"

"I don't typically stare." Her cheeks burned at the

admission, but hell, she had been the one to call him out for the same. Even if it was only a joke. "I don't want to offend—you have a very interesting face."

She had to stare up at him, then, as he rounded his desk and paused in his steps. He'd been reaching for something on his desk, but paused at the same time, giving her a quick look.

"An interesting face is one way to put it, Vera."

It was the first time he said her name; in his deep drawl, it felt commanding, accompanying a tug in her belly that she hadn't expected.

She couldn't stop herself from replying, "I never said that I didn't like it."

12.

She preened her throat-length bob often; as a nervous tic, she toyed with it or swept back the few wavy pieces of dark hair at the front of her oval-shaped face. Whenever she wanted just an extra second to think about her next words, or even every time he glanced to the side and found her staring at him again.

Vaslav hadn't expected that to happen. That if he *did* get her here, she'd even agree to stay. He'd been told before that he didn't exactly give off a friendly vibe.

His desire to meet the broken ballerina that had captured his attention was nothing more than a short distraction for the chaos that was his current life. He certainly hadn't assumed she would so easily agree to something like tea with a stranger, under otherwise shady circumstances. It wasn't as if he were a normal man who could approach Vera Avdonin in the way someone else might. He couldn't exactly bump into her at the coffee shop on the corner when every unplanned minute outside of his strict schedule could mean terrible consequences for him.

Or someone else.

Getting her there—for something as innocuous as *tea*—seemed impossible, and Vaslav figured that was where it would probably end. Except the woman showed up, dainty shoulders draped in what he bet was a buttery soft cashmere shawl. Beside him where they sat having tea, close enough that he could smell her. When she wasn't using loose strands of her hair as a distraction, she played with the fringe on her shawl.

He couldn't help but notice those little things, almost obsessively curious if he could find any more of her comforting quirks in between their quiet, safe conversation about the weather and house.

"This—" Vera tipped her small chin toward the cup she lifted for another sip. "I'm a fan."

"A man in Ontario, Canada makes it. He's … a bit of an artisan. I met him one day by chance on a business trip when I was stuck in between flights in an airport, and he gave me a few bags of tea."

Her ocean-blue eyes widened when she smiled. It was pleasing in a way that he would continue the conversation just to see if he could make her do it again.

It wasn't like Vaslav to share—hell, he'd ignored the first fifteen times his mother asked about the tea, and it took her a significant more amount of time to finally get her more recent answers.

"Those triangle bags smelled like coconut and cashews, and I was already in a mood," Vaslav added, readjusting his seat on the left side of the loveseat. "I forgot about them for a couple of weeks, stumbled on them one night, and then had to find the man to make me more because he'd been right."

Vera arched an eyebrow. "About what?"

Already, he'd offered the woman more information than he wanted to because it opened the conversation for her to ask more, and he hated giving people details. It was bad enough that he had to talk to anyone in the first place.

But he was quickly reminded that he'd asked this woman here—assuming she wouldn't even come— and because of that, he had no plan. No set way he intended for this conversation and tea to go, so that left him open and vulnerable to her soft-spoken question asked with a pretty smile.

"You don't have to answer," she said without warning.

Vaslav leaned forward to place what remained of his second cup of tea. "Most people choose not to point out my long stretches of silence when they have conversations with me."

"I didn't point it out … exactly."

He scoffed, hearing how derisive it sounded and not caring a bit when she tried to hide her wince. "Don't try to—"

"Complex people have complex thoughts. Sometimes that means they spend a lot of time inside their own mind, thinking or overthinking. Sometimes in conversations, they need a second or two to think. Either way," Vera said, lifting her shawl-covered shoulders in a shrug, "they almost always have the most interesting things to say."

The harsh, angry words he had planned to tell her to make sure she did not make the same mistake with him in further conversation died on the back of his tongue. He swallowed it down, but didn't find any bitterness left behind.

It wasn't often that he couldn't find words.

Vaslav was the first with words—*cruel*, swift words ready to cut, command, or cull. She called him complex and posed it as a compliment, but his medical history explained those lapses in his speech and time lost in his thoughts as something else entirely.

"What would you know about someone being complex?" he asked.

She considered that, her reply not as fast, and he took just a little bit of satisfaction in that. The woman had been terribly quick on her toes from the moment she walked into his den, but for the moment, she traced the rim of the teacup with the tip of her thumb in silence. He almost missed it, but just before she dropped his gaze, her stare fell on his hands. It lingered there, just for a second, on his tattoos and rings, before she focused on the cup instead.

"Personal experience," Vera finally replied. "It sits heavy in your stomach, doesn't it? The tea, I mean. I like how it keeps the nutty aftertaste, but it's almost like it … fills you."

How ironic, he mused.

He hadn't wanted to answer her question in the first place, and even deflected their conversation into dangerous territory, only for her to come up with the truth all on her own. In a way.

"It soothes the churning, empty feeling because of that—but only if I drink it in small sips, as it goes from hot to lukewarm. And it tastes good, of course," he added.

He didn't add that his digestive issues were symptoms of medications that were supposed to help with the pain. Sometimes they did, until it hit the magical threshold, and nothing worked.

"Of course," she echoed, glancing up at him again with a smile.

"I imagine I am not very good company—even for tea, no?"

Vera didn't bat an eye, and her laughter had a tinkling quality when she replied, "Well, I think you're only a little moody."

*

Vaslav loosened up a little once he was wandering the rear property line with Vera not too far from his side. She'd mentioned the sun dropping once, and he remembered that she would eventually have to leave. So, before she had even finished her second cup of tea, he offered to take her around the back of the house for a stroll, and they would come back to the front where he knew Igor was still waiting.

Vera agreed.

"There's a pond down in there," he explained as Vera leaned over the metal gate that kept a small dirt road blocked. "Once you walk behind the trees, and around the bend. Tucked behind the guesthouse, but it's rarely lived in now. I used to swim in the pond a lot when I was a boy."

Vera peered back at him over her shoulder, still beaming. How someone could smile as much as her, even in his constantly scowling presence, Vaslav simply didn't know. He found it fascinating, though.

Or just her.

She was interesting.

"How come you stopped swimming in it?" she asked.

Because I went to prison.

Vaslav swallowed back that answer, shrugging a non-response instead. She didn't seem bothered by it, and he continued walking on only to hear her footsteps padding on the grass behind him.

"Are you the one who cares for the lilac bushes out front—are you taking clones from the big ones, too?"

Vaslav nodded as she fell into stride beside him again. "Most of the time."

His only real interests and hobbies revolved around his home and property; it wasn't like he had the time, or patience, to find anything outside of it.

"It's beautiful here," she noted.

"A bit of a drive, though."

As they trekked up the small hill until the house came into view once more, Vaslav glanced down to find Vera walking along just fine. If her ankle was giving her any trouble, she didn't show it. He figured he'd done well not to ask about those things, or all the other information he had dug up on her since their first meeting.

Not without trying.

He had the strangest urge to ask her all the things—*anything*. Just to see if she might answer. She'd come there, after all, and while it had been less than an hour since her arrival, this was already coming to an end.

He considered asking her to stay for dinner as they came to a stop at the crest of the hill, but hesitated when she asked first, "You really only wanted to have me for tea?"

"And to say thank you."

Vera didn't ask for him to elaborate, and he was thankful. It wasn't often the words *thank you* crossed his lips—they could be a curse as much as they were a gift. He'd never thanked a man that he ended up killing, but he figured the woman grinning up at him, simply because she was happy that he asked her if she'd like to walk the property, wasn't quite the same.

"I can't offer much more, but at least this," Vaslav said, gesturing around them, "allowed me the chance to say thank you."

"I tried to ask Feliks if you were okay after, but he proved to be less than useful. Not that it's anything new for him."

The mere mention of that man's name was enough to send Vaslav's blood pressure skyrocketing. He'd never done well at hiding his inner irritation, and the disgusted sound that escaped him gave more away than he intended.

"Glad to know I am not the only one who thinks the man is insufferable," Vera muttered.

That caught Vaslav's attention.

"*Insufferable*—he's less than scum, no?" he asked her.

What on earth had the man done to earn this sweet, kind woman's anger and bitterness? He could see it in the way her mouth had set into a hard, grim line and even the tenseness under her eyes, like she was holding back emotion. He let her have that moment to stare out at the trees instead of him, he didn't need to see the entirety of her face for her profile to tell the truth.

Something *hurt*.

She was hurt.

By *Feliks*?

Instantly, that very idea made him irrationally angry, and Vaslav didn't have a single clue why. He'd be a damn liar if he said that knowing the man had done something to displease this young woman made Vaslav want to find out why and what, and make Feliks apologize.

That wasn't out of the question, either.

He only needed the time.

"Weren't you there to see him that day?" Vera asked. "Why else would you be at The Swan House? I think I would have noticed you before."

"Seeing a person doesn't equal enjoying their time, does it?"

Vera took another minute to respond, and he realized in that time that her personal experience in complex people was undoubtedly *herself*—maybe his pauses and long bouts of time spent unraveling the thoughts in his mind weren't because of brain damage like the doctors proclaimed. She did it, too, and clearly … the woman was nothing like him.

"You're right," she said, then. "I shouldn't have assumed. You know, Igor said I should mind the dog—Marrow? But I didn't even get the chance to see him."

He hadn't noticed until she mentioned the bull's name, but he could see Igor wandering around the west wing of the house from where they stood.

"Yes, that's a shame," he returned simply.

Although, with a loud whistle, the dog would come running within minutes from where he had decided to den in the nearby woods. The Moscow Water Dog was never far from his master, although one wouldn't know that considering how much time it seemed like the dog spent away from the house. Vaslav hadn't even fed the pup in years because Marrow did well to hunt wild hares and other small game all on his own.

He'd never met a dog before that scoffed at kibble—Marrow proved himself as capable and as vicious as his master on all fronts, including finding the food he wanted to eat.

Besides, when the dog did spend more time near the house ... it only meant one thing.

"Is he trained?" Vera asked.

"As a service dog, actually."

Of sorts.

Marrow had not been his idea, initially. Igor also hadn't given him much of a choice three years earlier after he'd heard a doctor's suggestion that a service dog might be beneficial to Vaslav. He'd brought the pup to the estate, mostly trained, at a year old. The woman that had accompanied the dog to work and train him with Vaslav didn't last longer than a couple of months, and Marrow hadn't worn his special vest since.

"Maybe you could meet him next time," Vaslav offered.

He didn't expect her to say yes or agree. In fact, he figured she wouldn't even turn her head to meet his gaze again to acknowledge the offer.

It wasn't the dinner he'd first considered, but it still gave him the chance to see her again, even if he knew that wasn't the best idea. This woman had better things to do than spend her valuable time with a man like him.

And yet, she stared him straight in the face with another one of her blinding smiles when she replied quietly, "I'd like that, Vaslav."

"Vas. You should call me Vas."

Vera nodded. "I will. Thank you for asking me for tea today. It was a good way to end a bad day."

He wanted to say the same, but the tendrils of pain snaking through his head had accompanied him since the morning. He'd known the bad migraine was on the horizon the second he walked outside to take his breakfast in the back, and Marrow was already waiting there to huff and puff his deep woofs along Vaslav's legs while he tried to keep down his food and morning coffee. He'd not seen the dog in two weeks—since the beginnings of his last spread of scattered migraines that remained for days. He'd staved off the current one for as long as he could throughout the day with drink and a handful of pills, but that didn't change what remained.

His pain.

"I'm happy to help," he returned.

She reached his way with her soft palm, covering his scarred cheek before he'd even comprehended what had happened. *No one* touched him. Not without permission, and not ever so suddenly that he didn't react first.

There was something about her touch, though.

He liked it.

Her thumb stroked over his beard before she quickly pulled her hand back, saying only, "Really, thank you. And I would like to do this again."

"Then, we will."

He'd make sure of it.

13.

"Mr. Pashkov?"

Mira's knocking continued once more on the outside of the den's thick doors, but he doubted that she would keep it up when she wasn't getting a response. The woman knew better than that.

"Mr. Ivanov just returned from taking the young lady home," Mira added, her voice muffled. "He thought you'd like to know she made it safe and sound."

He did want to know. In fact, Vaslav even gave Igor explicit directions as to doing exactly that because he'd not missed how Vera said she had been having a bad day. Not that it mattered much, now.

He swayed where he stood at the front of his desk, barely able to see through the double vision that had accompanied him since he returned from the outside. He thought he could get ahead of the worst of the migraine by downing what remained of the vodka in the last bottle he had in the den—that didn't work.

If anything, the liquor had settled too heavily in his stomach, mixed with the tea in his otherwise empty stomach, and the churning came back with a vengeance. Between the pain splitting his skull, the fuzzy, wavy vision making every step he took feel like the ground was coming out from under his feet, and the burning clench deep in his gut ...

Vas could barely breathe.

Let alone *think*.

He couldn't even remember how he came to stand at the front of his desk. Was it to get up out of the chair because he was scared that he wouldn't be able to later? Or had he not even been sitting behind his desk in the first place?

"*Jesus Christ*," Vaslav hissed.

He squeezed his eyes shut as tightly as he gripped the edge of the desk, trembling from the very tips of his fingers all the way down to his toes in his shoes.

Hell.

He was already in hell.

Vaslav hadn't even gotten undressed from his day clothes yet; didn't have the energy or give a damn to do it either when he knew by the morning, after his first night with practically no sleep, the clothes wouldn't matter anyway. Not unless he could find the motivation to strip and get under the spray of the shower.

As hot as it would go.

God, that sounded good. Anything would be better than what he was currently doing, really.

The chance for some relief sent Vaslav moving away from his desk. A mistake he regretted the second he took that first, wobbly step. There was something to be said about a man his size crumpling to the floor. It wasn't graceful; he barely had time to consider that he had been upright a moment ago before he was suddenly sprawled across the cold, hardwood floors.

On his back, Vaslav groaned while he blinked up at the ceiling overhead and tried to figure out what just happened.

He'd heard the crash of items around him, likely from his hand sweeping his desk. Something shattered on the floor along with his own body—he hoped it wasn't the crystal bowl that Irina had gifted him to hold the hard candies she once liked. Or even the priceless lamp with a mushroom-shaped shade made of stained glass, that had belonged to his great-grandmother and had been in this very room since the house had first been wired for electricity.

It was too late now.

Vaslav groaned out what air remained in his chest. The smack to the floor had taken the rest from him, and if those deep pulses of sharp agony in the base of his skull weren't so familiar, he might have thought he hit his head, too.

But that was just the migraine.

The knocking on the den's door had yet to cease. Mira must have heard him fall, but Vaslav couldn't respond to her calls when he was too busy trying to focus on the steady pulls of his short breaths into his lungs. It never felt like he could get enough.

Not quite.

"Mr. Pashkov! Can you hear me—are you okay?"

Somewhere outside, close to the windows of the den, Marrow howled. It was loud enough to make Vaslav think the sound rattled his bones. He hated that sound, if only because it reminded him of the pain inside his head. Every high-pitch howl licked his already bleeding brain with salt to cover the wounds.

"Get that fucking dog in the house!" he roared.

It was the only way Marrow would quit.

When he could lay his one hundred and thirty-five pounds of muscle in front of his master's door where he could growl at the slightest of movements within breathing distance of his massive paws. *That's* when Marrow would stop.

The howling continued.

So did Vaslav's rage.

He liked to think the pain was what made him mean—it could rip away his sense in an instant, and leave him a vicious, violent mess. But the vodka and pills didn't help when they only numbed his emotions and nerves but left his mind confused and robotic. Dull, and slow. Sometimes, he couldn't even hear his own yelling.

Vaslav managed to make it back to his feet, but his still-swimming vision didn't allow him the focus he needed as he stumbled through the ruins from his desk. Glass crunched under his every step while he pressed his fisted hand into the side of his temple because the pressure there felt like his head was about to explode.

Was Mira still knocking?

He wasn't even sure.

Igor wouldn't come near the den when his boss was already raging mad, so he didn't worry in that regard. Vaslav was alone with his pain.

For the moment.

He'd barely stumbled beyond the threshold of the bathroom down the hallway at the rear of the room when he started puking. His gut could only churn for so long before it began to rise. At least, he managed to make it to the bathroom this time.

*

The echo of soles slapping against hardwood dragged Vaslav back to awareness. Not that he had truly reached the blissful state of sleep in the past handful of days, but in that moment, he'd been close to it.

As close as ever ...

His peace was precious; nothing irritated him more than someone interrupting it.

"Mira said you were feeling better, yeah?"

Vaslav didn't respond to Igor's question, but he took in the way the man's footsteps lightened a bit once he was inside the den. Once Igor was close enough that the man's presence was beside his boss, he turned into a statue.

"Does that help?" Igor asked. "That on your face?"

The facecloth, he meant. Vaslav didn't even bother removing it to pretend like he *wanted* to have this conversation in the first place. After soaking the cloth with ice cold water, using it to cover his face from the nose up helped to soothe the remaining pressure pain as his migraine waned.

"We can do this another time, if you—"

"The door is open, isn't it?" Vaslav finally asked back, referring to his den doors, the words taking any breath he had left and leaving him panting at the end.

He cursed low and pressed his palm against the facecloth to give it a bit more pressure on his face. Unfortunately, the damn thing was already warm from his body heat.

Of course.

He did *not* want to get up again.

And no, he didn't want to talk, either. This was the least amount of pain he'd been in for … days. Nonetheless, he *could* form words and without dry heaving at every other sentence, so he might as well get this meeting with Igor over with so the two could move forward with their week.

"My bad," his head of security apologized. "I did see Marrow was outside last night, too."

Vaslav left out a sigh and reminded himself that of all his men … Igor was the most loyal; the only one that continued to have constant access to the man who ran Moscow's underworld of criminal enterprises. He never breathed a word about Vaslav's medical issues to people who may use it to their benefit, and he did every job placed into his hands regardless of the bloodstains left behind.

He's chatty, Vas told himself, *but if you have a friend here—he's it.*

"Made a damn mess of a hare in the front yard," Igor muttered to himself. "Mira loved that."

Vaslav almost asked if his man cleaned up the dog's first hunt after he'd finished a job well done—looking after his master—but he already knew the answer.

"I watered your shrubs along the front this morning, too. Been a while since we've had any decent rain," Igor noted.

"This fucking thing is warm again," Vaslav grumbled, pulling the facecloth away from his face. He regretted the choice immediately, because even though he'd pulled the shades in the den to prevent light from filtering in through the windows, there were cracks in the black velvet curtains. A few streams of light was enough to damn near blind him in pain all over again.

He barely had time to think about the facecloth that was pulled from his hand before footsteps carried further away from him, toward the rear of his den. Shortly after, water was turned on while Vaslav swore enough to make a priest blush as he pressed the heels of his palms into his face.

Igor returned to his side just as Vaslav dared to pull his hands away, only to find his companion had the facecloth cold, rung out, folded and ready for his boss's face. He said nothing as he placed it over Vas in the same way the cloth had rested before, not even acknowledging the fact he had done it in the first place.

The chilly cloth gave him relief all over again.

This time when Vaslav sighed, he wasn't even ashamed to hear the bit of bliss that slipped into the breathy noise.

"*Spasibo*," he murmured, the thank you so quiet that Igor only cleared his throat, but otherwise, didn't respond.

"Business?" the man asked.

Vaslav nodded.

Better to get on with it.

"The Italian has confirmed he'll move forward with the first run of cocaine into Moscow—"

"You mean to say he's finally done wasting time and has agreed to whatever you've put forth, no?"

"Essentially," Igor returned, unbothered.

"Perfect."

The bastard took more time than Vaslav had allowed. Lucky for him, the Russian boss was distracted with other things.

"After he sits down with you for dinner, and a chat," Igor added.

Vaslav scowled. "*What?*"

"Apparently, it's a matter of semantics—or theatrics. He doesn't like to work outside of his typical circles, and you're a new client, so to speak," Igor continued quietly. "Who the hell knows how Italians get any business done, Vas … all they want to do is eat and *talk*."

Igor wasn't wrong.

"Where does he want this to happen?"

"Paris, actually. He's willing to do it with the middleman, who made a very gracious offer to be no man's land. And we won't be giving the location to the Italians until a time of your choosing."

"When?" Vas asked.

"He'll leave that up to you, but preferably—"

"As soon as possible."

That's how these things worked. The faster Vaslav moved for the Italian, the faster the Italian would move for him.

"What else?" he asked Igor, still pressing his palm down flat to the cloth for the pressure. The kindest thing to have touched his face since Vera's soft hand …

"Your next appointment is—" Igor sucked in air, adding, "Well, I forgot. But Mira noted it down."

"Fuck the doctors."

"Vas, it could be serious."

"I said—"

"You've paid them a lot of money to run all of these tests. I know you don't want to hear it, but a part of you must have wanted to know why it's been getting worse, Vas, you ran for MRIs and every other

124

test they wanted to throw at you for months. At least let them tell you—"

"What I already know?' he asked under his breath, chuckling dryly. "Why bother?"

"You don't *know*, boss."

"Don't I?"

Igor didn't respond, and the seconds of silence continued to tick by.

"Dues?" he eventually asked his man.

"Paid, collected, and delivered from every brigadier in the country in lots of time, as always. The accountant has also taken control of all of the accounts Nico was funneling into for the brotherhood. Which means, it's about time for a body to wash up in the canal."

Vaslav grunted under his breath at that, offering nothing more.

Igor knew what he had to do.

Once every bank account across the world that Nico had been using to hide the organization's money was back under Vaslav's control, they had no reasonable reason to hide the fact that the man was dead—and had been for a while. He'd show up in the canal, wrapped in garbage bags and duct tape, but it would be too late for anyone to take what the man had left.

It would already be gone.

Back in the hands of the man who owned it.

"Speaking of Nico," Vaslav said, his words gravelling from the lingering pain.

"On that side of things, yeah," the man continued, not needing further direction from his boss, "Feliks has continued his daily life and business as usual. He's not mentioned to anyone that he's recently had no contact with your sovietnik, and he's gone about his days as he does."

"Another body that needs to wash up."

"Let me know when," Igor replied.

"If I even want him *found*."

"Well, dealer's choice."

"*Hmm.*"

"What?" Igor asked.

"How is the ballerina?"

Five seconds passed.

Vaslav counted each one.

"I was not aware I should be checking in on her," his head of security admitted. "And with the added pile of shit from Nico, frankly, I haven't had the time."

He appreciated the honesty.

All the same ...

"Make time," Vaslav uttered. "She's useful. Look at who she is, Igor."

"I have, and yes, her father has business with the fuck in Palermo, but—"

"If I had time to go through the information you provided about her enough to find the connections she has and how we could leverage them if needed, then so should you. You're going to have to be better about these things. I can't always fill in the blanks."

"Boss?"

Why did the man sound confused?

"Did I stutter?"

"Well, no."

Vaslav waved a finger over his head, not bothering to take the facecloth away so he could see Igor when he added, "Hell, maybe she'd even like to go to Paris—I do like to have a leg up when I can. Ask her."

"Might that be something you should ask her yourself?"

"Except you're going to do it for me."

After all, Vaslav *was* otherwise occupied.

He still couldn't get off the damn couch.

Before Igor's footsteps could creep away, Vaslav asked, "Is it Monday?"

It felt like a Monday.

"Tuesday, Vas."

Dammit.

He hated losing days.

14.

"Well?" Hannah demanded.

Vera couldn't even lift her gaze to look at her friend in the chat screen. "I didn't tell the kids I was quitting."

"I knew you wouldn't do it."

"*Actually*—"

"You've always had more class than that asshole deserved," Hannah interrupted.

Vera did smile at that. Her best friend wouldn't even breathe Feliks' name. She hated the man that much.

Understandable, really.

"But I *was* going to tell them," Vera said. "Sunday night, when I was talking to my mom, she said as long as I gave them time to make it right for the kids, find somebody yes, you know?"

Hannah nodded on the laptop screen. "Sure."

"Yeah, then it wouldn't be so bad. And it's not entirely on me if the company had time to replace me, plus I don't have to feel like I'm just walking out on the kids, too."

"*They* deserve you. That other thing, though …"

Vera only laughed.

It was still too weak, and her friend heard it.

"Sorry, Vera. I swear this is worse for you because nobody's there to help. I wish I could be there, but you know what Viktor would do to me if I stepped off a plane in Moscow after everything."

"I know, don't worry about me."

"I still do. You don't even go to the movies anymore. I haven't been able to get you to take time off since I moved back to Italy to be with Mom, either so it's not like you're traveling. Vera, you gotta do *something*."

Nobody asked her friend to point it out, however.

"I like what I'm doing, though," she replied to Hannah, adding silently to herself, mostly. She wasn't entirely able to keep the edge out of her tone. A defensive clip to her words that Hannah, the queen of passive-aggression, wouldn't miss.

And she didn't.

"Okay," her friend replied, twisting the word with her sarcasm and rolling her pretty green eyes on the screen. "When was the last time you even went out and got a good fuck from somebody, Vera? You don't even need to pretend to care about somebody to just do that. Jesus—wait …"

"What?"

"No, I had to think about it, but I don't think you've even been on a date since—"

"*Shut up.*"

Hannah rocked side to side with her laughter, and it was only her friend's wide smile that kept Vera from getting too in her feelings about the teasing. Truth be told, it was only once Vera met the woman—younger than her by only a year—at The Swan House that she loosened up a little. Hannah was good for that.

Vera sunk deeper under the chunky, woven blanket that she liked to snuggle with while she read and the television across the living room played some soap opera she didn't even like. That was her nightly routine, certainly nothing special. The occasional phone call she took from her parents back in the states, or Hannah, in Italy, was the extent of her current social life.

Compared to the hustle and bustle of what her social and nightlife used to be like, her current choice of relaxation and entertainment probably seemed pretty boring to an outsider. Even to Hannah, who never missed an opportunity to still enjoy the luxuries Italy had to offer. Especially to the wealthy, or well-known.

"I really am fine, even if I haven't had a proper date in a year," Vera said once Hannah's laughter lightened.

"He was rich, though."

"And married."

That was one problem with liking older men.

Hannah made a noise at that, considering before she replied, "For some people, that's not a problem."

"It is when he was looking for an arrangement."

"Again—"

"That included paying me, Hannah."

On the screen her friend tried not to smile. "Like I said, for some people, that might not be a problem."

Well, it had been for Vera.

Considering the way her personal and dating life had been complete shit before that last date as well, she hadn't been exactly hyped to get out and try again.

"What does it matter? There isn't a man in Moscow that could do for me what any one of my battery-operated toys can currently do, frankly."

"You sure?"

Hannah didn't know about Vera's trip the week before to have tea with the man in Dubna. The strange man, with a name she couldn't quite forget but had yet to whisper to another soul, who hadn't been too far from her mind since the night she rode away from his estate. Not his gorgeous, scarred face, their open-ended conversations, or his promise of another time for them to meet. She thought about him constantly.

Maybe too much.

"Yeah," Vera said, hoping her friend hadn't noticed the way she'd drifted off in daydreams for a minute. If she did, Hannah never said. "I'm pretty sure."

"You sound like the worst liar. Vibrators don't have hands to hold you down or a mouth to call you a dirty whore—I know what you get off on, and anything with batteries isn't only getting it done. It's not doing the whole thing, Vera."

"Go to hell," Vera joked.

The two women broke into a fit of giggles, one sitting in her Milan apartment, and the other, in her Moscow villa. She was grateful, at least, that the distance between them and the length of time they'd gone without seeing each other hadn't affected their friendship at the end of the day. Even as their laughter quieted and their conversation stalled while Vera scrolled through the options of the TV and

Hannah tapped away on the screen of her phone, she just enjoyed her friend's presence.

Even if it was only digital.

"I am quitting, though," Vera said.

"*Sent*, there. Ma can handle that. What did you say?"

"I am quitting, I didn't tell the kids and couldn't even go in yesterday because there was a water leak Sunday night inside the south wall of the studio. There won't be any classes for at least two weeks, so I couldn't give the kids the news, anyway. But I will … and I'm going to promise them I'll stay until after Christmas."

"The new year, then?"

Vera shrugged under her blanket, her attention drifting back to her friend on the laptop screen resting between her folded knees. "Feliks has until January first to figure something else out."

"Well, he can't blame you, and it's more than he deserves."

"True."

"So, are you waiting two weeks to tell him that, too?" Hannah asked.

Vera laughed. "Oh, no. I decided to tell him tomorrow. I heard he's going to be busy—it's his birthday."

She couldn't wait to ruin it.

"That's cruel, I love it," Hannah crowed.

"But it's a weekday, so he'll be there when I go into The Swan House. Might as well just rip that Band-Aid right off."

Hannah was still laughing. "I never should have retired. The drama was always the best."

"You retired before you divorced, Hannah."

Her friend winked on the screen, saying, "Yeah, but Viktor paid for that too, the prick."

Vera didn't doubt it.

*

"Is this going to be a regular thing?" Vera asked the man she found waiting at the end of her driveway later that evening when she stepped out for a walk. She posed the question to Igor after she had locked the villa, and finally noticed his presence.

The sky was just beginning to streak with pastel hues of the oncoming sunset.

Igor even had the nerve to smile where he leaned against the shiny black paint of a Range Rover. "What? I was just in the neighborhood and thought you'd like to see my new ride."

"I wondered if that was new." Vera eyed the car, appreciative of the rugged lines. "And that's the worst lie I've ever heard. You being in the neighborhood, I mean."

She liked the white accent lines on the matte black rims.

"How long have you been standing out here?" she asked.

The man shrugged. "Not long."

"You could knock on my door next time."

Igor's left eyebrow arched higher than his right. "There continues to be a lot of that between the two of you—this *next time* game, yes?"

Vera only smiled, but otherwise, didn't comment on the statement as she took the steps down from her villa's stoop two at a time. "What does he want?"

"How do you know he wants something?"

Vera came to a stop at the edge of her drive, just three short feet away from the towering Igor. She had to look up at him, much like Vaslav, but only amusement stared back from this man.

A *friendly* amusement.

She bet he was funny. He seemed like the type to be the life of the party if the timing was right.

He didn't, however, watch her with the same stormy-blue, piercingly haunted gaze that the man in Dubna did in his backyard while the sun set around them.

"Can I tell you something?" she asked him.

Igor squinted one eye down at her. "You didn't answer my question first."

"Well, how do you know what I have to say won't answer it?"

"I'm not much for the whole question for an answer thing," he returned.

"Guess you'll never know the answer then."

Igor finally cracked another smile. "You're fast with a reply—I bet that's why he likes talking to you so much. You don't give him too much time to think."

Hadn't she?

Vera didn't point her inner question out.

"Do you want me to tell you what I wanted to tell you, or not?" she asked.

Igor shrugged one leather-covered shoulder. "Lady's choice."

"He's still just a stranger to me."

"You've not even done a web search of his name, girl?"

Vera shook her head, unashamed.

"Maybe you are foolish, no?"

She wasn't offended by his comment.

Much.

"And I know he wants something because he wouldn't send you otherwise—I bet you have far better things to do. Probably for him. Believe it or not, but I still don't have a clue about who he is except that he's important ... and apparently dangerous. And I know that upturned spider tattooed on the back of your hand—and the one I saw on his—means you probably don't want me to ask a lot of questions. So, when I say that I haven't asked a lot about him, and I only know what I know, that's exactly what I mean. Which brings me back around to what he wants—you're here, so he wants something."

Igor slipped his hands into the pockets of jeans and rocked back on his heels a bit.

Vera stuffed her card wallet, phone and keys into the thigh pocket of her running sweats. "I'm working on a five-k run a day."

"How's that on the ankle—I might have seen something somewhere about that?"

Right.

"Easier than it used to be."

"Huh," Igor noted.

"What does he want?"

Igor sighed. "I should've just done this over the phone—he could have asked you himself."

"Better things to do, maybe?" she offered sweetly.

The man only glowered at her.

Vera smiled back.

"Paris—he has an upcoming trip next week, and he wondered ... maybe you would like to join him. It'll probably only be a couple days, maybe three at the most."

"For?"

"I'm not offering further details."

"I do work," she told him.

"Most people do, yes," Igor replied easily.

"Most people couldn't rearrange their schedule in just a few days, either."

"I'm not here asking other people, Miss Avdonin. I'm here to ask *you*."

Was it crazy?

Could she see Hannah if her friend had time for a short flight? Hannah never missed a chance to visit Paris, even if she could only stay for a night.

And him, she thought.

She would have time with Vas.

Maybe then, she could stop calling him a stranger.

"Would you be coming, too?" Vera asked.

"Another man will probably accompany Vaslav on his business trip to Paris; we're running a bit short on hands here in Moscow for people who can handle a certain subset of my boss's business."

"Oh, now it's a business trip?"

Igor only sighed.

Vera laughed back, walking down the sidewalk away from Igor without warning. "Tell him I'll go— I'm sure you can let me know when and where to be, right?"

"Vera!"

She glanced back over her shoulder to find Igor had turned to watch her head down the street. "What?"

"I'll knock next time, but I won't ever wait by the door for you to answer."

She stopped walking. "Why?"

"Because I already know he'd kill me if he thought

I stepped foot inside."

15.

"Vera."

"Alexi," she replied, opening her front door a bit wider when she realized who had been ringing her doorbell. "Hi."

The familiar man standing on her front stoop smiled wide. "Been a while, yeah?"

"That's an understatement," she replied easily.

"What's a handful of years between friends, huh?"

"I remember you telling me once—I think it was my seventeenth birthday after I went to a party—that you weren't assigned to me to be my friend, actually."

"Because your father wouldn't have hesitated to put a bullet in my head if he thought you believed we were anything *but* what we were, Vera."

She considered that.

For mere seconds.

"Fair enough," Vera replied. Shifting from foot to foot, she peered over his shoulder to see if anything or anyone waited on the street behind him, but she didn't see anything. "No car?"

"I thought a walk would be nice today."

The sun was out and high in a cloudless sky, but that didn't mean she trusted Alexi—a man who had once been tasked as her personal bodyguard hired by her father until she turned eighteen—to be honest about his sudden presence on her doorstep when they hadn't spoken in, quite literally, years.

"What do you want?" she asked.

Being straightforward almost always got Vera everywhere.

Alexi chuckled, his brown eyes crinkling at the edges a bit as he did so. "Just to have a chat. If you've got a minute, I mean. Then, I'm out of here, and you won't have to worry about me again. Promise."

Those few crow's feet around his eyes, and the bit of salt peppering his dark, short curls were the only signs the man had aged or changed since she saw him last. He still preferred his jean jackets, matching ripped denim pants, and combat boots considering his current outfit.

"You turned thirty-six this year, right?"

"Thirty-seven."

Vera nodded. "Right, well, do you want to come in for a minute?"

Alexi shrugged, and did a side-to-side check of the rows of villas on the street before stepping inside after Vera had moved back and opened the door wider. She intended to ask if he wanted coffee or tea, but when he remained lingering in the entry hallway after she had closed the door, she didn't bother.

"Not staying long enough to take off your boots?" she asked.

"Better not. And I have a ... an engagement later."

"So, a chat, then?"

"Right, let's get to it," Alexi muttered, shoving his hands into his jeans pockets. Only a couple of inches taller than her, she moved to be in his line of vision, so he didn't have an excuse not to look at her while he talked. But that didn't stop him from surveying the large piece of rolling luggage Vera had waiting in the hallway. "Going on a trip?"

"To Paris, yes. It's a … not a long trip. What's going on?"

Alexi sighed, turning his stare on her when he said, "You're aware that I still keep tabs on you and report them back to your father occasionally, right?"

Vera blinked. "Not exactly."

And she couldn't say she was pleased about the news, either.

"Demyan and I had an agreement about when I became an adult, and—"

Alexi tipped his head back and forth, quieting her instantly. "Technically, you got what you wanted. I wasn't within twenty feet of you every waking hour of your days, and you were welcome to have a life outside of his hand of control. No?"

"What exactly do you report back, and how often, Alexi?"

At least, the man had the decency to look ashamed.

"It used to be once a week, at first, but it turned to once a month, and now it's every three or so. It's not like you do a whole lot, Vera, you know what I mean?"

"*And?*"

He rolled his eyes at her defensive question. "Listen, it's not a big deal. He's an important man, who deals with dangerous people, and you're his daughter. I would think less of him if he *didn't* keep up to date with what was going on in your life, or who is in it, for that matter."

Vera's brow dipped in confusion. "Well, if you're only updating him, as you say, every couple of months—"

"Three."

"*Whatever*. Then you're not with me every day to know anything about my life, who is giving you the information, huh?"

Ask the right questions, get the right answers.

Vera played this game before with Alexi—she respected him for the fact that he *would* tell her the truth as long as she was smart enough to ask the right question to get it. This wasn't an exception to the rule.

And she was already suspicious.

Alexi cleared his throat. "Well, you see—"

"Who?"

"Anybody willing to talk to get a regular, small monetary payment that has valuable information."

She considered that statement, and what it meant. She rolled the words around in her mind, mentally flipping through the people in her life that could be beneficial to an arrangement like Alexi discussed.

"My neighbor?" she asked.

"One."

"Mr. Anatoly?"

Alexi barked out a short laugh. "*Right*, fuck no. That man told me to shove my money up my ass. To be fair, though, he keeps an eye on you. He did take my number, assured he'd call me if he thought you were in danger or something. Nothing else."

Good to know.

Vera was going to start paying attention to the other people near or dear to her life and those inside the small bubble of her world. She understood how her father justified his reasoning for keeping tabs on her while she was away from him, but the time for that was long over. And she'd made that clear when she turned eighteen, or so she thought.

Demyan had been happy to let her think so, however.

"What kind of things do they tell you?"

"Vera—"

"Just tell me," she snapped.

"If anyone has been around. If you're keeping your regular schedule. Any changes that might be important, or something new they noticed. Nothing serious or too personal, I promise. They're not the kind of people who even know those sorts of things about you, okay? It really *is* just to make sure you're safe away from the Avdonin family's reach and control. That's all. Except you never cared about that, you just didn't want people in your goddamn business, girl."

Vera let out a slow, steady breath to attempt to relax. It didn't really work.

Shocker.

"What are you doing here—that's what I want to know. Right now, Alexi. Or get out."

The man nodded. "Okay, so someone noticed you were having unusual guests. Strange cars parked out front, things left on your doorstep. I looked into some stuff, and found out that you had dinner with—"

"Tea, actually," she interrupted, her voice only a murmur. "I had tea with Vaslav Pashkov, and I'm going to Paris with him, but considering there wasn't anyone around to hear that conversation, I bet you didn't know about that."

Alexi let out a woosh of air, pursing his lips and staring Vera down. "That is a dangerous man, Vera."

"Any worse than my father—my brother, or grandfather? Or you, even. *You* have the stars on your chest, don't you?"

Alexi didn't even blink. "It's more than that, Vera, trust me."

"Let me guess, you're here to warn me?"

"I came to chat."

"*Why?*"

Because she kept asking that.

She didn't think he'd answered it, yet.

Not truthfully.

"Let me put it this way—this situation you find yourself in, I mean," Alexi explained, lifting one shoulder and letting his gaze drift back to the luggage in her hallway. "You know how your father would hear if someone so much as breathed wrong in Little Odessa—all of New York even, I'll give him that."

"What about it?"

"The man you had tea with owns every dirty and bloody rouble in this country, Vera. You think the tattoos you can see on his hands tell you a story?" Alexi rocked back and forth on his heels, leaning closer to her when he chuckled and added, "Vera, what you can see about him is the *warning*. I don't even know how you managed to find your way into his company—"

"Luck—or not, considering."

"Considering what?"

She thought about Vaslav's fall; about how those

around him didn't want to acknowledge it had happened, and how even he refused to engage any mention of it with her after the fact. She certainly wasn't going to discuss a man's private business with just anybody.

Even if that anybody was Alexi Volkov.

"I ran into him one day in the city. He sent someone to ask me over for tea. It really is that simple, and there's nothing else to it."

Alexi glanced down at the luggage. "And now you're going to Paris with the man?"

"Looks like it."

"When you make a deal with the devil, Vera, he owns you forever."

She wasn't concerned.

"I'm nobody to Vaslav Pashkov, Alexi. I'm not worried about it."

"Wrong."

"I'm sorry?"

"Have him tell it, and I bet Vaslav would say every person he's ever let into his world is somebody to him. There's a reason he graces them with his attention, after all. No matter what form that attention takes. Trust me when I say, there are men who would prefer they didn't have his attention, and you're a woman who's about to jump on a plane to Paris with him, apparently. How do you think I know he's the goddamn devil?"

"Are you going to take this back to my father?"

"In two weeks—when he expects my next update—yes. That's what he pays me for."

But that wasn't why he was here.

She'd finally figured that out.

Vera nodded. "You're giving me a head up, then?"

"And a warning. He *will* be concerned. Nature of the business."

"And you are, too."

"Pardon?" Alexi asked, arching a brow.

"You're concerned. About my involvement with Vas."

Alexi didn't acknowledge her shortening of Vaslav's name. "Vera, they don't call that man The Beast of Moscow because he's spent his life doing amazing things. They call him that because they've never heard or seen a more violent, unstable bratva boss in this country's history of criminals. He spent most of his youth and adult life inside prison walls—inciting gang riots for shits and giggles—and for the last decade and a half, he slowly took over a criminal empire. Do you understand that?"

Well, she'd suspected one of the things Alexi revealed—Vaslav's connection to the brotherhood, the Russian mob—based on the upturned spider tattooed on his hands and the other inked rings on his fingers. The rest?

That was all news to her.

"I hear it."

The man groaned under his breath. "Yeah, right."

"I do hear you—I just don't think it's relevant to spending a bit of time with him. I am capable, and *will*, make my own choices about my life. Like I always did."

"Fine, don't say I didn't try, Vera. It was good seeing you."

"You don't have to lie, I know I always pissed you off. Papa must pay very well."

Alexi rumbled a laugh under his breath as he headed for the door. "You just didn't like to listen."

Not much changed, then.

"Hey," she called when he reached for the inside doorknob on the door.

He hesitated, looking back but saying nothing when he raised his brow.

"He's like them, I understand that."

Mafiya, she meant.

Dangerous.

She'd known men like that her whole life.

"But you miss the point that he's *not* them, Vera. He's not a man who loves you, or even cares about you, and that's where you might find a problem."

"I'm still going to Paris."

Alexi nodded, replying just as fast, "And I will still be filling your father in."

16.

Igor standing with his arms folded over his chest as he surveyed the private tarmac of the airport shouldn't have been a concern for Vera when she stepped out of the black town car. But it was a crease of worry she'd seen on his brow as he stared at the small, commercial jet fifty feet away from where her driver had parked.

"*Spasibo*," she thanked the driver, still leaning in the rear door.

Igor was already coming her way, reaching for the trunk of the car to lift it when the driver popped it open.

"No worries," the man replied in Russian, smiling wide at Vera. "Have a lovely flight."

The driver had arrived on time, loaded her bags without complaint, and didn't scare her half to death on the drive to the small, private airport just outside of Moscow. What more could she want?

The wheels on her luggage clicked to the smooth

asphalt. In a quick jerk, Igor had extended the arm of the luggage, and then he spun it around to offer the end of the handle to Vera. She took it with a smile.

"Thanks. It's good weather to fly."

Igor squinted one eye to the bright sky. "If only the weather mattered at this point."

He said it so low that with the wind rushing past, she almost didn't hear it at all. Despite wondering if that was his point, she couldn't ignore the worry that reflected in his gaze when his stare dropped back down from the sky to her.

"Something wrong?" Vera asked.

Igor's attention darted beyond her shoulder to the white jet with the black and gold detailing. "It's been a while since he's traveled without a companion, that's all. I'm not used to being the one who stays behind, yeah?"

Vera smiled. "I'll be his companion."

He didn't even crack a grin. "Not the kind that carries a gun."

Fair enough.

Vera figured she'd also asked enough.

"I better get going."

Igor nodded, stepping back. It was the first time she noticed how formally he was dressed, right down to the light blue vest and tie under his black suit jacket. "Right, he certainly doesn't like to wait. You have everything?"

"Everything I was told to bring."

"And the driver filled you in—"

"On the flight plan and your number, should I need it. What *would* I need it for, exactly? I meant to ask …"

Igor tapped the bottom of his throat with two

fingers she said, "You'll know. If you have to use it."

Well, then.

For the first time, even after her former bodyguard had showed up at her place the day before with his own warning, Vera felt those familiar pangs of unease deep in her gut. Alexi's warnings had felt almost hollow to her.

"He's good to fly, right?" she asked. "I mean, I don't want to ask about his medic—"

"*Da, nyet.*"

Vera quieted instantly.

"Don't," Igor added. "And it wouldn't matter if he could or couldn't—the fact here is that he *is* flying."

She was ninety-nine percent sure the man wanted to add *because he said so* but opted not to. The tone of his voice gave it away.

"Enough of this," Igor muttered with a nod at the jet. "Get going."

"Any rules this time?"

Igor did smile at that. "Go on his cue?"

Why was that a question?

Vera didn't bother to ask.

*

The jet leveled out lower than Vera expected it to, and she couldn't help but notice the way the wing tilted to the left a bit when she peered out the porthole window.

"They're circling back around—I wanted to fly over the city before we left."

"Why?" Vera asked the man in the white leather seat across from hers. The small jet had the same color scheme on the inside as it did outside. A vast amount of luxurious white with crisp, clean gold and black accents on everything from the seat belt and buckles to the cupholders in the four rear passenger seats.

She hadn't gotten a chance to really check the plane out when she boarded because as soon as she did, a flight attendant directed her straight to her seat. They taxied shortly after, and Vaslav didn't even bother to say hello. Never mind put down the *Moscow Times*, one of the few newspapers that retained some semblance of control outside of the government. That tended to happen with media that had connections to the mob.

Or so she had heard.

Vera didn't care to know if it was true.

"Can you see the canal yet?" Vaslav asked.

He hadn't even bothered to answer her question. In fact, he still hadn't put down the newspaper creating a thin wall of gray, black and white between them. Vera tried not to be annoyed by his lack of attention, considering *he* asked her to come on this trip with him. Then again, he'd barely grunted at the flight attendant when she asked him to put away the paper before takeoff.

Clearly, he didn't listen.

"I hope there's something interesting to read in there," Vera said before she could stop herself.

"Actually, there is."

Without warning, Vaslav folded the newspaper back together and dropped it in the middle of his lap. She would have been happy to finally see the man's face, except his eyes were covered by opaque aviator sunglasses. The furrow of his brow and hard-set line of his squared jawline gave very little away except that he probably wasn't happy.

It was hard to admire the rest of him, every inch of him filling out a black-on-black suit and the dark silk shirt underneath his jacket that had been unbuttoned at his throat, when all she could make out of the man staring at her was his scowl.

Was it because of her?

Vera hoped not.

"Do you like flying?"

Vaslav released a woosh of air, tipping his head toward the porthole window, leaving his scarred cheek facing her instead. "Not particularly, but it's sometimes a necessary evil."

"Igor wasn't happy to be left behind."

That didn't earn her much of a response.

Vera tried something else. "I also found the perfect spot to plant my lilac shrub this spring."

Vaslav turned her way again.

She didn't even hide her smile.

"Oh?" he asked. "Tell me where."

"I always wanted to put something right in the middle of the backyard where I could put a bench. It'll be all sun, all the time."

"When it's out," he agreed quietly. "A bench would be nice."

Tentatively, and only because she had the man talking, Vera said, "You seem … tense today."

Or maybe different.

"It's an important day."

"Because you're going to Paris?"

Vaslav shook his head, leaning back toward the porthole window where he pointed out for her gaze to follow. "There's the canal, see …"

"Why were you looking for it?"

He didn't even miss a beat. "I heard a body was

found today."

Vera's gaze snapped to his, but she couldn't see anything beneath the opaque lenses, and even his scowl had retreated for the moment. The man truly was unknown to her—in many ways. It should have been a red flag to her that she knew so little about him, yet he felt magnetic just sitting across from her on a private jet.

Except the warning only made her all the more curious.

She peeked at the paper in his lap.

Was that what he'd been reading? Vera didn't get the chance to ask.

Vaslav leaned back in his seat, tugged the aviator's off, and managed something of a smile for Vera. The chill his words had created low in her spine had started to crawl its way up her back, but it was gone the moment he turned his attention on her.

"So, you have three and a half hours, yes?" he asked.

"For what?"

"That's the length of this flight."

She hadn't even realized.

"So?" she asked.

Vaslav chuckled. "You'd think you might have something to say or ask me."

"Do you want me to ask you things?"

"I didn't invite you on this trip to talk to myself." Readjusting his position in the seat, he unbuckled the belt before the light overhead had turned off to signal he could do so. Then, he unbuttoned his jacket and relaxed a bit more. She still thought his tall, well-built frame seemed tense across from her. "Frankly, I invited you because I needed a companion on this trip when I *do* want something to do, and at this point, my only other option was my mother."

He practically spat out the last word.

Vaslav shook his head. "I'd rather knife my fucking eyes out."

She couldn't stop her nervous laugh, but he grinned all the same at the sound.

"I'm not exactly sure what we're going to be doing," Vera said. "I have a friend flying into Paris tomorrow morning so we can get together; she's been my best friend for years. I don't have any other plans, and since I was told I could do whatever I wanted, I didn't think you'd mind—did you?"

"Call it a work trip," he returned. "I won't do much else, but there's a purpose for that."

Vera scrunched up her nose, amused. "One I suppose you won't tell me?"

A chuckle escaped him. "*Net.*"

Of course.

"What's your favorite memory?" Vera asked.

The man across from her practically turned to stone. "I think you've taken enough turns, *kisska*, if you don't mind."

Vera tried to focus on the fact he'd quickly diverted a more personal question at the same time her body decided to react to this intensely overwhelming man calling her a kitten. With a baritone that her hormones decided to notice. "How do I resemble a kitten?"

"All fluff, no claws."

"Screw you."

Vas smirked and his gaze darted to the side where he could see the familiar city below. Low, he uttered, "Anything is possible."

Or at least, that's what she thought she heard.

Vera couldn't be sure.

"What is *your* favorite memory?" he asked.

She didn't even have to think about it. "I was three—my father took me to a museum, and there was a portrait of a dancer that was as tall as the wall. Imagine how big it looked to my eyes. I did my best version of her pose; I think my father even took a picture. It's also one of my earliest memories."

"I can't actually remember mine. Not first-hand, anyhow." Vera blinked at the unmistakable sadness that coated Vaslav's unexpected admission. Yet, as fast as it was there, she didn't hear a drop left behind when he added, "Was that when you knew—that you wanted to be a ballerina, yeah?"

Vera swallowed the lump of emotion forming in her throat, wishing it was easier to nod. She managed it, even whispering, "Most likely."

"You were crying the day you saw me fall in the gallery, weren't you?"

The next flutter of her lashes sent two small teardrops racing down her cheeks. He barely glanced her way to notice, but he remained unaffected at the sight of her sudden tears all the same.

"I can't remem—"

"Oh, I bet you have a far better memory than me, Vera," he said, almost *chidingly*.

She squirmed in her seat.

Uncomfortable, and liking it.

More than she should.

It was a strange thing, to be sad and turned on at the same time. Vera couldn't particularly say it was her favorite, but her emotions quickly swung to the more painful side of things when Vaslav asked, "You *were* crying, yes?"

"And dancing; sometimes I do both, now."

"Pity—broken *and* sad."

Vera winced at the cold and flat way he delivered those words. They weren't necessarily untrue, and she should be unsettled at how intimately he seemed to know her history, but mostly, she chose to stay silent. It wasn't easy.

Vaslav sighed. "Was that cruel? I can't ever tell."

"A little."

"Mmm, that's just your raw nerve, *kisska*. People tend to irritate those when you least expect it."

Vera blinked again.

More tears fell.

"Is it that it hurts—physically, your ankle, I mean, yeah—or something else?" he asked.

She didn't need him to clarify. "The last thing I felt when I danced professionally was shame. It was the only thing I felt; I couldn't tell you from what. From all of it, maybe. The failure, the publicity, *my* injury; knowing after—"

"And now that's all you feel when you dance."

Vera tore her wet gaze away from the porthole to find he was staring right at her again. Now that she knew he was, it was as if the heart in her chest could feel the weight of his gaze, and it started thumping harder.

"But I wish it wasn't," she whispered.

"See," Vas murmured, gravelly and bored, "still broken and sad."

She wished she could be as unaffected as him.

"Nobody said you had to point it out."

"You'll never fix it if everyone lets you pretend it's not even there to begin with," he returned.

Or was he just the only one who had seen it?

17.

Have you landed?!

The text was accompanied by ten different emojis ranging from heart eyes to wide smiling faces and even a bottle of popped champagne. Hannah's excitement at being so close to Vera, the closest they had been since her friend left Moscow, was palpable in the messages.

Vera kept peeking down at the phone in her hand—that message from Hannah waiting on her screen—but she still couldn't reply.

Not yet.

Eventually, the screen went blank.

Vera could have been doing a lot of things except standing at the rear of the three-story apartment, watching the man in the sunroom through the panes of glass shout into his phone. Hell, on the other side of the apartment was a great view of the Eiffel Tower. She didn't even have to go out on the stone veranda to enjoy it because every room at the front had more than enough windows to allow the guests the particular pleasure.

Instead, her feet were cemented to the floor, and she couldn't look away from Vaslav. Not that she could hear what he was yelling—he'd shut the door to the sunroom, and she remained far enough back in the hallway that she could see him, but she didn't believe he could see her.

It left her with only the muffle of his voice.

Enough to know it was raised. The contempt and anger twisting his expression with every word gave it away, too.

How fast things changed …

The thought almost taunted her.

Vera tried to shrug it off, and the warnings that had found their way to her in various forms since her first meeting with Vaslav. That was harder to do when she couldn't look away from the proverbial train wreck happening in front of her.

All I did was ask a question, she told herself while Vas paced the sunroom from one end to the other. It'd been mostly a joke. He'd not stopped the pacing for the entire twenty-minute phone call. She knew he was raging in Russian because of the little bit that she *could* hear, but otherwise, she couldn't quite gain the courage to cross the space between the short hallway and the sunroom at the back.

Not that she was scared he might yell at her—even if he did, it wouldn't be the first time a man had raised his voice in her proximity.

That's not what stopped her.

She could still hear Igor back in Russia warning her.

"Go on his cues?"

She'd missed a cue.

A ballerina that couldn't hit her mark.

The second the question had left her lips as they stepped beyond the small gate protecting the apartment building where the driver who'd picked them up at the airport parked, Vaslav's entire demeanor changed in a blink.

"Why do they call you the beast?" she'd asked.

He was laughing, then.

At something else she'd said while they exited the vehicle and waited for the driver to pull out both bags that took *way* too long to be checked at customs. The moment his laughter died on his lips, and suddenly, he wouldn't even look down to grace her with his gaze, she could *feel* it.

How cold he became.

How fast his muscles turned to stone.

In fact, he'd altogether walked away from her, not even leaving a chuckle behind. She'd raced to catch up as he crossed the cobblestone pathway leading to the apartment entrance they were meant to use. She'd barely had time to admire the yellow stone that made up the outside of the building, or the lush green ivy vines crawling all the way up to the red mansard roof. He'd given her so little information about the place— she actually thought they would probably be staying in a hotel for the duration of the trip.

Vas wouldn't talk while he unlocked the door, and she asked about the apartment—was it his, rented? Did he know the owner? How many bedrooms?

She got nothing.

Vera didn't need to be told to know she had fucked up here—*somehow.*

Did that qualify calling Igor—he said she would

know if she had to, and Vera felt like now was the best time. Stepping back a foot in the hallway, Vera leaned against the yellow painted plaster wall, resting between two paintings of an ocean view over jagged cliffs, as she found the contact number she'd previously punched into her phone.

The instructions from the driver who had taken her to the private airport had been clear. *Don't put his contact name as his real name. Give it a nickname, if you want.*

So she had.

Funny Man

It felt appropriate, but Vera didn't have an ounce of amusement in her when she called his number. Putting the phone to her ear, she did her best not to chew on the side of her manicured thumb nail while the call rang through.

Except he didn't pick up.

Three rings in, it went to voicemail.

Vera tried again.

Same thing.

She considered leaving the hallway and finding her bag, changing into something more comfortable, but they'd rushed inside so fast that she couldn't even remember the layout. She'd been too busy chasing after an angry Vaslav who refused to speak to her or explain what was wrong when she figured out something *was*—how was she supposed to know she should remember the three levels of room, hallways, and stairwells to get back down?

Frustration was Vera's greatest enemy. It was *just* an apartment—one with a beautiful view, and easy access to everything that was great and wonderful about Paris. She could easily navigate her way through the place, if the frustration she experienced just being there wasn't so overwhelming for her.

She didn't like to struggle, now. Vera had a bad habit of questioning herself and choices when it was accompanied by the prospect of success or failure.

How are you succeeding or failing here? It's not like you're on a stage here three seconds ahead of the count, Vera.

She didn't even have an answer to her own mind's question.

One last time, Vera tried to call through to Igor—and this time, she stepped closer to the end of the hallway where she would have a view of Vaslav once more. The half-partition wall made up of plaster on the bottom and windows at the top looked into the sunroom that appeared to take up over half of the third floor's square feet. He'd stopped pacing, at least, where he had planted his feet shoulder width apart in the middle of the room. He even took off his suit jacket, so she had a view of his tense, muscular back. One fist held his phone to the side of his head, and the other remained balled at his side.

Still pissed.

The call rang only twice before it ended this time, leading Vera to believe that Igor was simply rejecting her calls manually. Almost to the second it ended, she watched as Vaslav's head tipped to the side. He turned slightly, enough to glance over his shoulder in the direction that he had used to enter the room.

Straight through the windows to *her*.

"*Go*," she watched him say.

Whether he shouted it, or simply mouthed the words, she understood.

Plain as day.

Vera squeaked under her breath, unable to contain

the surprise before she spun on her heels and took off down the hallway. Maybe this *wasn't* the right time to call Igor.

So, when was?

*

Vera had explored the better part of the bottom floor by the time her angry companion decided to make his way back downstairs. She'd skipped over the bedrooms on the second floor as she figured that was a bit too close to the pacing man upstairs.

Her favorite room, after the kitchen painted in the same yellow tones that was fully stocked with food, was the den at the front, across the hall from the large dining room that led into the kitchen. Big bay windows overlooked the quiet street, and the better part of the upper half of the Eiffel Tower could be seen beyond the rows of homes across the cobblestone street.

In front of the bay windows sat a glossy white piano. She didn't know how to play, but she could already hear the keys tinkling away while the tower was lit up at night.

"He means when I am dead," she heard spat behind her.

Vera spun around on her heels, away from the beautiful view beyond the lush, shimmering curtains framing the window. Vaslav stood in the entryway of the open den where the hallway and stairwell was in view. She hadn't even heard his footsteps coming down.

"I'm sorry?"

"Igor," Vaslav said, the name clipped in his mouth.

"When it comes to his number, you should use it *only* if I am dead. That's something he'll want and need to know in regard to you and me. Otherwise, I will provide you with a number to use to call should you need something he isn't required to provide. Do you understand?"

Vera's brow rose slightly. "Did you not know he had given me his—"

"No."

"What?"

"Is an explanation required?" he asked back cuttingly.

Vera blinked at how mean he could sound without even trying. He stood there stoic, gaze cold and hard, but he delivered his words with a tone so cruel it stung upon impact.

"I didn't ask very much about this trip—in fact, I didn't even ask for it," Vera said quietly, doing her very best to be unmoved by his aura of aggression. Maybe he didn't mean to come off that way, or perhaps he meant exactly that, but she wouldn't be intimidated by it. "So, maybe you can understand why I would use the phone number provided to me when you decide to act like a spoiled child instead of telling me what I did wrong."

His chin tipped up.

Not much, but it did.

She took his moment of silence as a chance to speak again while she had the chance.

"It was a joke, Vas," she said.

"Except someone told you it, and when I tell you it's not the name they printed in papers, or hollered at me in the streets; it's *not* a name they call me to my face, it means you had to learn it from somewhere. I

163

want to know where."

Vera fidgeted under the weight of his stare and her growing silence that followed his demand. Eventually, she asked, "That's why you called Igor?"

"I thought he let it slip—he's done it before with you. Talked more than he should."

"He's *nice*, and probably does his job well, from what I know."

"Which isn't very much," Vas bit back.

God.

Even his teeth clenched now.

Vera sucked in a gulp of air, setting her jaw in a line by gritting her teeth. "What is your problem?"

He took a step forward, and then another. Another few, and he'd be close enough to reach out and grab her, if he wanted. He didn't come that close, but his energy and that heaviness he carried around with him became all the more pronounced to her in that moment. More palpable in his anger, she bet it could swallow another person whole.

She could understand why someone else might step back when he came forward. Why they might want to bow to him, in some way, submit to his very presence. In another circumstance, maybe she would have, too.

But what had she done wrong?

Really, *what?*

Vera stood tall, chin up, gaze locked on his, and wouldn't budge, asking, "Well, what?"

"Let me make something very clear to you, yes," Vaslav murmured as he pointed a finger her way. "I understand you may have questions; accept that I will rarely answer them. My trip here is a carefully planned event—even the passport I handed over was chosen out of a stack, *kisska*."

Honestly, Vera figured she'd been kind not to look surprised as they were taken through customs, and the officers, with their French accents, questioned Vaslav using a name she didn't recognize.

"You are welcome to do whatever you like for the next forty-eight hours, as long as you are here to be picked up when the driver arrives on the third day. Other than that, you needn't ask or know anything else, and you won't even have to see me in between if you so choose."

"Why even bring me here, then?"

What was the point?

Vaslav only grinned—a bit. It didn't tilt the scarred corner of his mouth enough and left him looking all the meaner when he did it. "Because you're useful."

"What?"

What did that even mean?

"And find a new question," Vaslav replied as he turned around to leave. "That one gets boring fast."

18.

She thought he forgot—or maybe that he decided not to push—but that was far from the case. Vaslav had not missed the way Vera didn't hand over the name of the person who disclosed his infamous moniker, but one way or another, he would find out who let it slip. Oh, it was fine and great for him to say he was a beast; it wasn't quite the same when others did it behind his back.

If they wanted a beast, he could show them one.

Nonetheless, he'd opted to let the young woman stew in her feelings about the incident because that was the better option for him. For now. Everyone learned eventually ...

He never once said he liked the fucking name.

Vaslav hadn't expected to smell a hint of cigarette smoke floating down the stairwell, but he decided to follow it once he had. He was surprised to find Vera swinging in the freestanding, woven hammock with the cause of the smell dangling from between her manicured fingertips.

She even had French tips.

When in France, he mused.

Even in his head, he was dry.

Vera didn't notice his arrival to the apartment's upper sunroom—there was also one at the bottom, rear of the house attached to a private office. It led out to a stone desk and pathway through the rose garden at the back. He couldn't see her eyes hidden behind the sunglasses as she pulled another long drag from a red filtered cigarette, and he chose not to notify her that he was there for the moment.

Once he did that, who could tell how this would go.

After yesterday ...

While the smoke would usually do wicked things for his lingering migraine, he didn't mind when he got to enjoy the way her lips hugged the filter. A picture-perfect pout—ready for a kiss. She was close enough to the windows that she was able to just reach over and flick the ash out.

Maybe it was the sight of her stark-white yoga pants and matching sports bra that contrasted with the sun-kissed tone of her skin, but Vaslav suddenly understood why Vera would have been the wet dream of every man in Moscow back when her pictures were being splashed across every tabloid magazine.

Hell, she looked like his wet dream.

Actually, the one he'd had last night.

That was some bullshit. He couldn't remember the last time he'd had a wet dream. Probably when he was a teenage boy, sleeping on a cement slate with a blanket for a mattress. It was as humiliating now as it had been then—but good Christ, Vera had been a sight in his dreams.

The way the stretchy fabric hugged the slender curve of her hips and the small swell of her breasts proved his imagination could still do worthy things.

Vaslav blamed his current situation—mostly the semi-erection he'd walked around with for most of the morning—on the fact his pain had been lower on the scale for the better part of the week. He always had too much time to think, or apparently fantasize, when he wasn't in constant agony.

Even better when he could sleep.

"That's a terribly filthy habit for a former professional ballerina who I just saw come back from a run a while ago," Vaslav said.

He decided to let her know he was standing in the doorway where she'd left the door open against the wall. At least, she had opened a couple of windows for the smoke to travel out. Not enough, considering he'd still smelled it.

Vera didn't even glance his way, nor did her sneaker-covered feet move to suggest she was going to exit the hammock. "I allow myself one a month—I feel like I get to enjoy them that way."

"Maybe I can understand that. There was a time I bartered extra pieces of bread for a hand rolled cigarette to take the edge off before the lights went out, after all. Those were the days."

She did turn her head his way at that statement. "Like ... prison?"

A grunt of agreement escaped his lips, but Vaslav was already moving on to another topic.

"Oh."

"One a month isn't bad," he said, opting to fill the silence because he still couldn't see her eyes, and he didn't know how she had reacted to that statement.

Yesterday, he'd blown up at having something personal about his life shared. Now here he was, offering it.

"I let myself have two this month."

He didn't miss the bite in her tone for a minute.

"Because of me?" he asked, curious but he was sure he knew the answer.

"If the shoe fits," she might have mumbled.

Vaslav allowed her the slight.

He might have deserved it.

"Keep the windows open for a bit longer, yeah? The friend who allowed me to borrow this place for a few nights while he visited the Riviera isn't a smoker. And if I have to listen to the man bitch, I might just stab my eardrums out."

In the process of lifting the sunglasses from her face, Vera's hand froze at the top of her head. "You do hear how stuff like that sounds, right?"

Vaslav nodded. "That's the point, *kisska*."

"Huh."

"How was your run?"

She took another drag of the smoke, and this time, he forced himself to avert his gaze, so his mind didn't have yet another snapshot to take with him straight to hell.

"Pretty good—I ran to the tower and back, bought a bear claw from that little shop down the street, and almost rolled my ankle stepping off the sidewalk outside of the house," she finished dully.

"Does that happen often?"

"Only when I forget my fucking wrap."

Even the knot in her brow, when her face scrunched a bit in her disgust, was cute. And he immediately regretted that word passing his mind.

Now that he thought about it ...

He couldn't get it away.

"And you did?" he pressed, not that he had any business to. "Forget the wrap, I mean."

Vera sighed. "Yeah. Otherwise, I'm good to run three or four times a week."

"Just no eight-hour practices in pointe shoes, I assume."

"Basically."

"Don't you have a ... friend coming?" he asked.

"Hannah."

Ah, good.

He'd been sure she told him the friend was a her the day before, but he couldn't remember for sure. At the very least, his jealousy—a recent thing he couldn't say he liked—was controlled knowing she would be spending her day with another woman while he walked the apartment's floors mentally trying to rid himself of his semi-erection.

"I'm going to meet her in a couple of hours. And don't worry, I'll pick up any butts, too," Vera said.

"*Spasibo.*"

Turning on his heels, he decided to leave he alone again. After all, he'd promised not to be a nuisance while they were there.

"I really did only mean for it to be a joke," she called at his back.

Vaslav didn't turn around, but he did stay rooted to the spot when he replied, "Everyone likes to call me different things, and that is only one of them. Nobody ever decided to ask what made me that way, or accept their hand in it, in some cases."

"Raw nerves," he heard her murmur.

He smiled to himself, liking that she'd taken that phrase of his to heart.

"One of many for me," he returned.

"I'll try to keep it in mind."

A wise choice.

"Enjoy your visit with your friend," he said as he headed away. "And for what it matters, your casserole dish …"

Was Shepherd's Pie casserole?

Or pie?

Vas wasn't sure.

It didn't matter to how it tasted, either. Not that he had the culinary skills to make it himself, anyway.

"What?" Vera asked, and he swore he heard the hammock's bars creak like she had moved.

Her confusion made him chuckle.

Vaslav let his voice carry back to her as he entered the hall. "The supper you made last night. I found the plate you left me in the fridge. It was delicious."

Even cold.

He couldn't figure out how to turn on the stove or run the damn microwave to warm it up that morning when he'd stumbled on it. She hadn't needed to cook; an entire stack of take-out menus from restaurants that offered delivery—on top of the popular fast-food options—waited for her in the middle of the dining room table.

Instead, she had taken the time to cook. Finding everything she needed between the cupboard, fridge, and freezer. And she'd even considered him enough to plate him his own food whether he sat down to eat it with her or not.

That was why he came to speak to her after her run; why he followed that scent of cigarette smoke to the top of the apartment where he found her looking like heavenly sin in the hammock, kissing the end of a cigarette, and wishing it was his fingertip instead.

She had cooked for him, it was delicious, and then he felt like shit because she'd done all that even after he'd been a prick.

Vas wasn't one to feel guilt, and if he was mindful not to lie, he'd have to say he probably wouldn't feel it for very long. While he did, he might as well put what conscience he apparently did have left to use, even if he hadn't technically apologized.

Better yet, maybe she'd make him more food— then *he* wouldn't have to put those damn menus to use, too.

"I liked it a lot," he added as he reached the stairwell. The cheese on top made it perfect. "Next time, I'd like to try it hot, no?"

It took a second.

Her soft echo eventually came, though.

"Sure, okay. I won't be here to make something tonight, but the rest is still in the fridge. In the dish under the tinfoil."

Good to know.

19.

"How's the head?" Igor asked, his Russian smooth over the phone.

Vaslav appreciated—if nothing else—the fact that the man could ask the right question without asking the right question. "Nothing unbearable."

He expected Igor to press the issue. Maybe even ask a more direct question regarding his boss's pain level while he was currently out of reach, but Igor didn't. Well, not then.

"Pierre has a nice place there, yeah?"

"I appreciate his willingness to work with my demands," Vaslav replied instead of directly answering the prod Igor tentatively pushed him with.

"How many times are you going to use him for a middleman before you just agree he's worth the cost, Vas?" Igor asked quietly.

Another good question and considering the work Igor had been putting in for the bratva's business since Nico's unfortunate end, it was a question he didn't mind being asked. He had a lot on his plate—brigadiers to mind, collect from, and handle issues on top of his security duties between Vas, and the rest of the organization. Adding the responsibility of the brotherhood's money on top of a large pile, and they found themselves in their current situation.

Igor staying behind so no one knew an especially important man was missing and wouldn't cause issues—while Vas headed alone to a meeting made possible by a middleman who seemingly proved himself trustworthy.

So far.

Until Igor managed to vet every man he intended to work with, inside or outside of Russia, through Vaslav when it came to business, the man's plate of responsibilities would simply stay full. There was no other safe way.

Not without his enemies or rivals—or even the snakes in Vaslav's own grass—seeing the openings they had to a throne that he'd taken out from under every one of their feet without barely even trying. Some called him a king; others said he was a beast. Neither meant he was beloved.

Far from it.

He'd never forgotten it, either.

"Forever," Vaslav finally admitted. "It feels like I'm waiting forever to prove people are worth anything at all to me, Igor."

That wasn't the answer Igor had been looking for, and his responding silence gave it away. Oh, well.

Vaslav came to stand in front of the white piano with the gold trim that faced the bay windows. With the heavy curtains around it, he doubted someone from the outside could see too far in, and he felt safe enough standing beyond the stream of light cutting through the middle where the fabric was pulled open by rope with tasseled ends.

Gold and yellow everywhere.

He made the place more bearable by shutting every curtain or blind there was and turning off all the lights. Vera hadn't seemed to mind and used the lamps in any given corner when needed.

"The apartment is very … *bright*," Vaslav settled on saying. That felt as good as anything. "Otherwise, it serves its purpose. Couldn't say I would enjoy it as much if the Frenchman was here, too. One other person breathing in the room next to me is enough, you know?"

"*Otva'li*," Igor cursed.

"Excuse me?"

"Not you—the damn dog. He knows when you're not around, Vas. He's torn up the front lawn again; there's holes *everywhere!* You know Mira about broke her fucking ankle last night using the water hose?"

Vaslav sighed and scrubbed a hand over his scarred cheek that had been twitching on and off for the better part of the afternoon. His fingernails tugged into the hard scar tissue, and the nip of pain it caused stopped the tic almost instantly. There wasn't very damn much he could do about Marrow, so to Igor, he asked, "Was there anything in the papers today?"

"Only a small column that a body had been found."

He nodded absentmindedly to himself, satisfied with that for now. "Make sure you have a paper for me tomorrow when I step off the jet—I better see Nico's name in print."

"They won't hold it back for too long, boss."

175

"*Mmm.*"

His grunt went unanswered.

"Everything is good on my end," Igor said after a quiet moment had passed. "I'll send the Italian the meeting details at the time you specified, and the car will be at the apartment tomorrow at ten. Your longest wait is gonna be on the tarmac waiting for clearance."

Yeah, it always was.

"Right, well, you can tell my damn dog I'll be home tomorrow."

Igor barked out a laugh. "He barely comes out of the forest when he's in a mood, the stupid fuck. He just howls and howls. The *politsiya* did a drive through of the area this morning … the bastards. If it's not one thing, it's another. You've got to let me get someone on this property to clean a few things up, and get it ready for the winter before it's too late."

They had time.

And who cared about a few holes in the fucking lawn?

Vaslav scowled at the mention of police being near his home. "Knock on some doors, no?"

Someone had called to complain, after all. They wouldn't make the mistake a second time.

"I'll deal with the damn neighbors."

Igor always did.

Too bad someone hadn't been there to deal with the nosy bastards on the day they called the police to say he was beating a man to death. Would have saved him a lot of time in prison.

"*Vas*," came a loud call in his ear.

Blinking out of his thoughts, he realized when he looked down at the tips of his leather loafers, that

he'd been standing there long enough for the
sunshine to move a bit over his shoes. "What, Igor?"

"You didn't hear me."

"Things on my mind," he returned in a murmur,
knowing the man wouldn't question it.

Partly.

"I said, or asked rather, how's your other
roommate?"

"Out—coffee at a cafe, dinner later, and then an
evening under the tower, or that's what I heard her
discussing with her friend before she left. She's stayed
out of my way; it's been fine."

"Just fine? You almost bit my head off—"

"We'll revisit that conversation," Vaslav said,
referring to Vera slipping his moniker, "once I figure
out who told her. I thought I made myself clear on
that?"

Igor quieted instantly.

Maybe that was why Vaslav hadn't heard the man
ask his initial question. He almost didn't want to talk
about Vera—or the fact that he hadn't stopped
thinking about her since she left earlier to go meet
with her friend and the outfit she'd walked out the
door wearing.

She distracted him.

It was as good and welcome as it was a problem.
Or a possible one.

"She tempts me," Vaslav said.

Just because he *didn't* want to talk about Vera had
no bearing on whether he should. Igor needed to
know anything that posed a threat of sorts to his
boss, and a distraction could be exactly that.

Not that Vera herself was the threat.

Igor cleared his throat. "She's young—I think

people call it *vibrant* … she's quick on her feet, can actually carry a conversation, and pretty. I'd be surprised if you didn't look at her and like what you saw, Vas."

"Kind way of saying you think she's attractive."

"A *respectful* way."

Well said, he mused.

"But she's mostly just useful," Vaslav added after a few seconds. "And that's what I like about her the most."

Igor didn't reply.

His boss didn't really mind.

Even he could hear his own lie.

"You know, if you're bored," Igor said, "I could always call Veronika. I hear she's been living in Paris for the last year—thirty minutes, and she could be there."

Vas didn't so much as blink at the suggestion of his favorite escort being on speed dial, and available. She was a warm body, and a beautiful one, that had occasionally warmed his bed after he lost Irina; mostly because she started as his massage therapist, but she had a way with those damn oils. "I haven't seen her in over a year."

"I kept her number when she skipped out of Moscow; she told me to keep it just in case. She used to help you when it got bad, Vas. Might still, yeah?"

He considered it.

Just not for long, though.

"I have other plans tonight, Igor."

"Boss's choice."

It always was.

20.

There was something about the very sight of Hannah Malone's freckled, smiling face that could turn any day around for Vera. Maybe it was the way her friend's emerald eyes almost glittered when she was happy, and her whole aura—from her bouncy steps to her head of frizzy red ringlet curls—radiated joy constantly.

The woman made it hard to feel anything but happiness. Without even trying.

A person couldn't deny Hannah a thing, not if they spent any reasonable amount of time with her simply because of her sweet personality and friendly nature. There was no one more helpful; not a soul in the world more kind.

As far as Vera was concerned, anyway.

That was why the second she laid eyes on her friend after not seeing her for months, and the first thing Hannah did was smile in her big, bright way that showed off all of her straight, white teeth, she almost burst into tears.

Well, she might have shed a few.

Hannah let Vera hide them in the shoulder of her cream silk blouse while the two hugged next to the patio table in front of the cafe where they'd chosen to meet up. For the first time in over two years, since Hannah had met, married, and left the man she called her husband, there wasn't a bruise to find on her.

No healing, yellowish fingerprints on her arms to tell Vera her friend had been squeezed so hard Viktor had left marks behind again. There weren't any dark circles, or even caked on concealer to hide a lack of sleep or another punch to the face, when she'd pulled off her large-framed sunglasses to greet Vera.

Sometimes, she'd excused it.

Other times, Hannah had outright lied to Vera.

And anyone else who dared to ask or try to help when Hannah pulled away and her husband's controlling, abusive behavior became more apparent to the people in her life.

Then, Viktor had almost killed her. Vera would never be able to get the image of her friend's raccoon-bruised eyes staring back at her from a hospital bed out of her head. That memory, and every lump and bruise and cut on Hannah's body after that beating, were reminders of *why* she had to get away.

The subsequent divorce and Hannah's secretly chartered jet out of Russia in the middle of the night once the ink was dry had left Vera stranded, in a way. Not a *bad* way, because Hannah absolutely needed to leave, but it was all so fast.

"We didn't really get to say goodbye, did we?" her friend asked.

Vera pulled away from Hannah's hug with a

shuddering exhale of breath that belied the tears she'd wiped away as fast as they came. "You always know what I'm thinking."

"Since that day you sat on the studio floor across from me and asked if I was Irish, yep."

Her reply was typical, golden Hannah, too.

"My father is, but that's just what the DNA said, so."

Vera later learned that Hannah did spend a portion of her youth with her father's family, but he wasn't in the picture much.

A burst of nervous laughter escaped Vera. "You called Tony a shite."

"He was!" Then, Hannah stepped back a little more from Vera, and gave her high-waisted, sky-blue skinny jeans and white knotted crop-top a look. She didn't linger for long on the pointed toe flats Vera had pulled on to match her top. "I like it—still no heels, though?"

"Kitten only—"

"And only for special events," her friend interjected with a nod. "See, nothing's changed."

That was easy for Hannah to say, and honestly, Vera understood why she would want everything to just … go back. Back to a time when things were different before she'd met Viktor—or maybe before he'd changed.

Too much had happened for that, though.

"You're okay, right?" Vera asked.

Hannah smiled again. "Yeah, I am. Coffee, and then we're finding somewhere new for dinner, right?"

"Can I get another hug first?"

Her friend's arms were already opened, and the shorter, pixie-like woman launched herself straight at Vera ready to swallow her whole. Her hugs were as great and as warm as her smile. Too big for her small size, stronger than anyone knew, and *safe*.

Vera had never understood how someone who proclaimed to love Hannah could stand to hurt her or make her cry.

"I miss you everyday," Vera told Hannah, her words muffled against their tight embrace.

"Me, too."

Vera left the rest of her feelings unsaid; they weren't really needed, and she already told Hannah exactly what she thought and felt a long time ago. Long before she divorced Viktor and fled Moscow for Italy where her mother was waiting to be a haven.

She only wanted her friend to be happy and safe, and Hannah finally was.

Nothing else mattered.

*

"We're doing breakfast tomorrow morning anyway, right?" Hannah asked, swinging around where she sat on the wooden bench only fifty feet away from one of four feet that made up the bottom of the Eiffel Tower. "Why don't you just stay the night with me at my hotel?"

"I could," Vera replied, tossing what remained of her ice-cream sundae into the trash bin.

The thing about her and Hannah?

They liked to eat.

A lot.

Almost all of their activities and travel over the day included some kind of snack or treat to try. Hannah had even gone as far to create a map on her phone for the two to follow like a scavenger hunt of sweet and savory treats.

Paris style.

Or rather, *Hannah* style.

Taking the other side of the bench to sit, Vera crossed her legs and leaned closer to her friend to see the picture Hannah offered on her phone. The shot of Hannah standing on mossy green cliffs with raging waves at her back had Vera's heart skipping a beat.

"You look happy," she said.

"I was. Do you know how slippery moss is?"

Vera nodded, sitting straight again as Hannah tucked away her phone. "Slippery enough to know I wouldn't have stood that close to the edge for a picture."

"You never were a risk taker."

Well ... Vera didn't necessarily believe that. Her risks simply didn't look the same as others. Not that she bothered to say so—Hannah knew; her comment hadn't even stung a little.

"Anyway, I could stay with you tonight," she said, bringing their conversation back to Hannah's original question. "The driver won't be there tomorrow to pick me up until ten, I think, so—"

"Speaking of which," Hannah jumped in to say with a grin.

The glow from the lights on the lit-up tower overhead almost haloed Vera's friend to make her seem even more like an angel when she posed her next question, "You haven't said very much about the friend you came here with ... how come?"

"Not for a lack of you asking."

Hannah didn't even look a bit ashamed. "*And?*"

"Too bad we didn't make it over here before sunset to see the tower light up, huh?"

She even turned away from her friend as she made that comment about the infamous iron lady in hopes that Hannah would get the point. Vera just wasn't talking when it came to Vaslav, whose name her friend had not yet even learned. There wasn't much to tell anyway.

"Stop it," Hannah groused, "you're not even playing fair."

"There's nothing to play."

"Nothing to tell, you mean."

Vera shot her companion a wink.

Hannah scrunched her nose up right back.

"There really isn't much to tell," she admitted while the two watched a group of loud friends walk directly under the tower, never stopping their laughter during their stroll.

"There must be something, Vera. You flew— *chartered*—with a man who you're also sharing a private apartment with while you're here, and you don't have anything else to tell me about it?"

Nope, that was about it. Vera hadn't given Hannah anymore information to go on about Vaslav, or the unexpected trip to Paris that allowed the two girlfriends a chance to catch up. It was obvious to Vera that Vas was peculiar ... and maybe a little particular ... about his business and life; he took his privacy seriously, and she wouldn't share more than he had made it clear she was allowed.

Even to her best friend.

"We had tea," Vera offered quietly. "Once."

Hannah blankly stared back.

Vera eventually glanced away with a laugh. "What?"

"Was the tea *good* at least?"

"Nutty, mostly."

But not in a bad way.

"Vera!"

"What?" she asked again.

"You know that's not what I meant."

"Well, that's what you asked," she returned just as easily.

"You won't even tell me his name?"

"It's definitely not Viktor," Vera replied.

"Damn good thing, too."

Their quiet giggles were only hushed when the sound of rolling tires drew Vera and Hannah's attention to the crowd pushing a large piano over the stone walkway closer to the edge of the tower. Before long, a violin's whine echoed over to their spot while the other handful of people who had been moving the heaviest instrument began to pull other cases off the top and started to set up. The classical sound the group created attracted more people milling around the immediate area and before long, they had a crowd.

"Are we getting music *and* lights?" Hannah asked, beaming Vera's way. "The whole show."

She smiled right back. "I think so."

"I wonder if they'd mind if we danced. You'd waltz with me, wouldn't you? Don't make me find a stranger, Vera."

"Hannah ..."

The warning was for nothing, though. Vera knew it before she said it. Hannah had a way of getting everything she wanted.

21.

Finding her in the crowd wasn't difficult. Even if Vas hadn't known what to look for to draw his eye to the middle of the square under the tower, she still would have been hard to miss. A temptation made up of glowing skin and a twinkling smile with every laugh that passed her painted-red lips. She showed off a great deal of that porcelain skin with a sleeveless white droptop that was knotted between her breasts.

With blue skinny jeans painted-on-tight, and hourglass curves swaying in a fast dance with a tall redhead, why wouldn't people look?

Every man in the square certainly was.

Even him.

It was just too damn bad he also wished he was the only man able to see her dressed the way she was, dancing so freely, and offering her smiles like candy to anyone who got close. Vaslav came from a different time, from different men. He'd seen a woman get beaten for wearing more clothes than

Vera had on currently, but it wasn't her lack of modesty that had awakened the monster gnawing on his back, colored entirely green.

It was that the men in the crowd watching her—maybe even a handful of the women, too—wanted her. But if he acknowledged that it irked him as much as it did, then he'd have to admit *why*, just as well.

Vaslav didn't like *wanting* things—never mind saying so. He had so little self control when it came to something he didn't have but wanted to; how ironic that a woman twenty years his junior could suddenly turn him, a man who hadn't even as much as dated a woman on a steady basis before he married, into a jealous mess without knowing she was doing it.

He'd learned over his lifetime that some people were magnetic without trying, and others, without realizing—whatever energy made up their being or soul was something that drew other people in. Whether or not the people they drew in were good or bad was dependent on too many factors to count, and honestly, Vaslav was only looking for an excuse to look away from a dancing Vera being watched by a crowd.

His constantly chaotic thoughts were simply the excuse he decided to use. Too bad it didn't last for long.

Vaslav knew at his second look that he paid too much attention to Vera when he was able to notice from more than fifty feet away, while she spun and laughed under the lit-up tower with an equally joyful—and pretty—woman, that her bob was longer. The dark, sleek strands that had once been cut sharply just below her jawline had grown enough to nearly brush her shoulders. Which only drew his attention to the naked, delicate column of her throat, over her bare shoulders, and before long, he was devouring the woman across the way with his gaze again.

Maybe the fact that he believed Vera was one of those magnetic people was the excuse Vas could use to explain the urge he felt to seek her out, knowing she might be here because he'd heard her mention it during a phone call and nothing more. Maybe that was the reason he could lie when faced with his obsessive, almost compulsive, need to see her. And not just to see the woman—laying his eyes on her was only part of the equation. No, he wanted to watch her. Study her when others were around; take in how her mannerisms and expressions changed when she didn't know he was nearby.

Who was she when Vera thought Vaslav wasn't looking?

It wasn't exactly something he could ask.

Really, he wasn't the kind of man who asked for anything.

She was only supposed to be useful, but not also interesting. That made things terribly tricky.

Too late, his mind taunted.

The same mind—that at the same damn time— told him he should be doing a million other things. Better, more important things than stalking a dancing, young woman under the Eiffel Tower. In fact, the almost viciously sarcastic voice started making a list, and for a second, he wished the migraine he'd been provoked with that morning would return.

If for nothing else, to wipe out his thoughts.

Unfortunately, that didn't happen.

Even staring up at the bright lights spread throughout the tower did little to flare the pain he'd woken up with that slowly faded over the day. Lights were not his friend—natural, or otherwise. Yet, he felt nothing more than a dull, pulsing ache in his temples and a bit of uncomfortable pressure behind his slightly squinted eyes.

Vas should have headed back to the apartment only a short walk away, but it was rare that he was near a crowd of people who didn't know his face while capable of coherent thoughts untarnished by his pain. He wasn't about to waste it.

As he passed along the outside of the tower, something red caught his eye leaning against the back of a bench. The rose looked like someone had just placed it there with the intention of going back to it, but considering no one was around, he plucked it up as he moved on by and twirled the long stem between two fingers.

Considering the summer months usually brought more tourists to France, and specifically the tower, he wasn't surprised that as the time neared ten o'clock, a rather large crowd gathered in the area. He was sure the live, free music and pretty, dancing women helped. Although, one could tell the difference between the tourists and the those who would consider themselves Parisians quite easily.

One group couldn't put down their damn phones, after all.

He weaved in and out of a group of young twenty-somethings, one of which stood back from his group of friends to take pictures of their tongues stuck out and peace signs held high. How *cute*.

He could almost vomit.

Not that any one person got too close to Vas as he walked closer to the outside of the leg of the tower.

No one met his gaze for too long, not once they saw the right side of his face and the scowl that rarely left his expression, and they stayed out of his way as he moved through. As people usually did.

The high whine of a violin followed the end of the makeshift band's song, and the crowd's applause echoed up the tower and into the air like a megaphone. For once, a suddenly amplified sound didn't irritate Vaslav to the point of instant insanity.

Or rather, instant rage.

His oldest friend.

Instead, he was too busy staring at Vera again, and the redhead she was currently encouraging to say yes to a dance with a young man who'd approached the two. Was that the friend—was the redhead *Hannah*?

He really should have made Igor check up on those things, but the details of Vera's side excursion with her friend in Paris hadn't interested him enough to do so. Until now.

Funny how that worked.

The piano and a man working the cello started to strum out a slower tune as Vas came around the side of the tower leg. Vera must have been able to convince her friend to dance with the young man because she headed away from the two with a wave over her shoulder. Her lack of attention caused her to nearly run into an older lady who was asking a man to take a picture of her and her husband.

Vera's soft apology was accepted with an easy laugh by the woman and man, and something he couldn't hear them say made her laugh again. When she side-stepped the people and turned his way, her gaze finally landed on him.

Only twenty or so steps away, Vera's laughter died

on her lips, but her smile spread even wider. Sweeter, truly.

"Vas," she said. Still a little breathless from her earlier dance, her skin tightened over delicate collar bones with every inhale she took. "Did you know I was going to be here?"

"I was out for a walk, actually," he lied smoothly.

If she didn't believe him, Vera never said.

"Did you want to dance, too?" he asked.

Mostly because the slow, waltzing tune was the only thing he could dance to, and now it seemed like Vera's friend was busy with someone else.

Right, he said to himself. *That's why.*

"Are you asking me to dance with you?" she asked back.

He couldn't remember the last time he danced, but he knew when it was all the same. He had the details, but not the actual memory of his small wedding reception. It'd been years, either way, but he didn't hesitate to hold an open palm out to Vera.

"If you want to, yes," he told her.

She took his hand, grinning when he tugged her a step closer. "I'd love to dance with you, Vas."

*

"Is that for me?"

Vera's question drew Vas's gaze to the rose that he managed to keep captured between his fingers even while he held her hand high in his own to dance. "I found it, but it's just as well—it might as well be yours."

He continued leading their steps, and without missing a beat, twirled Vera away from him while he used his free hand and his teeth to snap the stem to a third of its previous length, leaving only the red petaled bulb and bit of green behind.

"No thorns," he told her. "I checked."

Vera's cheeks flushed with a light pink when he captured her hand in his own again and pulled her close once more. Their dance stopped just long enough for him to place the rose behind Vera's ear, tucking the stem along strands of her hair to keep it in place. Another time or place, and Vas would have been too concerned with the amount of people around, and the fact he was in public, but it was easy to push those lingering worries away when a beautiful woman couldn't look away the closer they stood.

While his fingers at the shell of her ear lingered, his other found hers to hold like they had been before. Her fingers wove with his, and her left shoulder lifted higher than the right as she let out a soft sigh when his fingertips brushed her cheek pulling away.

She wanted to dance, he reminded himself.

Except she inched a bit closer, and instead of putting his hand back to her bare, mid-back, Vas ghosted his fingers over the curve where her neck met her shoulder. Even when her skin pebbled under his light touch, she was still as soft as silk.

"Are we dancing?" he asked quietly.

A part of him wished she would say no. The part of him, beyond the cracked veneer of coldness and malfeasance, that had seen the way her breaths picked up and how she responded physically to being touched by him.

Say no, he wanted to say, *and let me take you anywhere; let me taste you everywhere.*

He couldn't get the words out.

192

Or she nodded before he could and caught his wrist to pull his arm back around her body. She still let him lead their steps, their waltz creating a circle around the outer edge of the tower's leg. Just far enough from the larger part of the crowd where they weren't drawing any significant attention.

Although he kept a featherlight touch where his palm and fingertips graced Vera's skin and spine at her back, he swore he could still feel the heat soaking from her body to his. Like electricity shooting straight through his fingertips, keeping them connected even if his hand barely put any pressure down.

"Who taught you to dance?" she asked.

"They offered a class in prison. I took exactly one."

Vera didn't bat an eye at his mention of serving time, but it wasn't the first, either. "Was that all you needed?"

"The basics are just that—basic."

"Can't really argue with that," she returned.

His dark chuckles accompanied the tempo of the song picking up slightly. He led their steps accordingly, and Vera, unsurprisingly, never missed a beat. She might not be on the stage dancing anymore in full traditional costume, but once a dancer … always a dancer.

Even if only to waltz under the Eiffel Tower.

She was all straight lines, grace on her toes, and a wide smile with every step and twirl. He couldn't look away.

To ignore the rush of lust that kept washing through his gut every time he met Vera's gaze, making him want to lean in and taste the red lipstick painted on her lips, Vaslav asked, "Are you letting your hair grow out again—it used to be long, no?"

"I haven't actually made time for a cut, that's all," she explained, "but maybe I'll let it grow again. I could do more with it when it was long, that's for sure."

"The bob fits your face, too."

And her pixie-like features.

Vera laughed. "Believe it or not, but it used to be curly when I was little. I had a whole headful of black ringlets until I started straightening the hell out of it."

Somehow, the picture of a young Vera in her childhood, with a head of wild, unruly curls, made him smile. He bet she had been a curious and precocious child—clearly talented and driven, as well. The way his muscles pulled upward on the scarred side of his face was so unusual that for a second, it felt strange.

Wrong.

He knew the way it made the crevices of his scar more prominent; how the jagged ridges became even more prominent. And yet, Vera just smiled back.

She didn't look away from his face, but it was like she didn't see anything but his eyes. Unaccustomed to someone holding his stare so blatantly for so long, Vaslav took the chance to let Vera swing away from him again, spinning under their raised hands before she drew closer. With his hand at her back, he kept his gaze locked over her shoulder as she held on to the side of his neck with her soft palm.

"You could have just said what you wanted to," he heard her whisper.

"Pardon?"

"Instead of asking about my hair. You could have asked what you really wanted to ask."

He cleared his throat, keeping her close enough

that she had to turn her head to look at him, but he didn't look back.

"What do you think I wanted, then?"

She didn't even think about it before saying, "To kiss me."

He almost missed a step.

But not quite.

"Or," Vera added quickly, "even that you liked it when you touched me, and that you might want to do it again. Or maybe, Vas, that you noticed how *I* liked it when you touched me."

Most people who had come in and out of his life couldn't manage to crack the safe that was Vaslav's mind. No one ever knew what he was thinking—they couldn't get past his severe expressions, long silences, and his usual disgruntled nature to figure out there was actually a constant stream of conscious thoughts inside his head.

This woman did it without even trying.

He liked that too much.

He liked too much about *her.*

Vera Avdonin was dancing with the devil, and she didn't even know it. If he was a better man, one with honor or morals, he would have told her as much.

Oh, well.

The song ended faster than Vas expected it to— this time with a zip of piano keys from one side to another as the string instruments came to a stop. The clapping encouragement of the crowd sent the band into yet another faster, jazzier song. They practically had their own stage for the night, as long as they kept playing. He stepped a long stride back from Vera before he asked her for one more dance.

And humiliated himself because he couldn't dance

to something like the makeshift band was currently playing.

"You should get back to your friend," he said, not meeting her gaze. "It seemed like it'd been a while since you saw her; I'd hate to interrupt more than I have."

Vera's soft smile faded a bit, right along with the twinkle of happiness that had been in her eyes. Her tongue peeked out to wet her parting lips, like she was considering saying something, but he didn't give her the chance.

Turning on his heel with a wave, he said back to her, "Tomorrow—ten for the driver."

"Right, but Vas—"

He hadn't seen the woman walking sideways with her phone in her hand and her focus on the screen instead of her direction until she slammed into the side of him, and he had to catch her fall. His Russian curse fell on deaf ears, because the woman apologized in clear English, as he helped her to her feet. Except he was just as much at fault because he was distracted with getting away from a conversation that had his stomach in knots with anxiety.

What was he doing?

"Apologies," he said as the stranger turned to face him.

She had been laughing it off, about to say something else to him when her eyes finally found his face when she was righted and okay. The moment she saw his scar, she was quick to glance away with a muttered, "Sorry, again, thanks for helping me, sir."

The woman scurried back to her female friend that she'd been trying to capture a picture of at an odd angle, apparently. Letting out an annoyed sigh, he turned to Vera with a rueful smirk and opened his arms wide, saying, "See, I really shouldn't even be outside."

Vera's brow pinched when she said fast, "Don't do that—or say it like that."

Her indignation at his desire to joke about his sometimes-frightening appearance was endearing and disgusting at the same time.

"Just because it isn't funny doesn't make it untrue."

Vera tipped her chin up a bit. "It's not a joke when it's at the expense of yourself; not when it hurts you. How's that funny?"

"Who said I was hurt, Vera?"

His flat delivery of the question would have been enough for someone else to toe the line, but Vera didn't back down. In fact, she had the nerve to cock an eyebrow when she said, "I didn't take you to have a complex, Vas."

At that, he barked a laugh.

"Or maybe I have one too many," he returned.

"No one wants to be seen as a monster."

As he turned to leave, determined to leave his ego intact, she called his name one more time. There was a damn good chance Vera only did that because she knew it would get a reaction from him. Nobody else would dare to do it so blatantly; he'd had the lesson beaten into much bigger men than her before.

Vera didn't know any better. "I bet you did want to find me tonight; that you asked me to Paris for a reason. I didn't take you for a coward, Vas—or at least, I didn't think you were the type of man to be afraid of telling a woman he wanted her."

Pride was a *suka*—a complete bitch on her best days. Today was one of the worst, apparently. Vera dared to call him a coward, and like a bolt of lightning had shot through his feet the second the words left her lips, his body had already decided to turn around before she'd finished her sentence.

How dare she.

How dare she assume anything?

She barely had time to see him coming. Vas crossed those few feet between them and moved on her like an eagle did when it swooped down on its prey. Swift, entirely sure, and right on the mark, talons at the ready. He wasn't kind about the way his fingers curved around her neck, both hands fisting into her hair when he yanked her head up. There was no softness in the kiss he crushed down on her perfect, red mouth, those small but lush lips of hers trembling open when his teeth dragged down the flesh. He felt the heat of her breath pulse against his mouth a second before his tongue darted past her lips for a taste.

Hot sugar.

She was like hot sugar on his tongue, and once he'd gotten a taste, he dragged her even closer to keep her from pulling away. There was something too perfect about the way she just took his kiss—submitting to the roughness with brushes of her own lips and ragged breaths she couldn't control.

He wasn't scared for her to know that he wanted her; that wasn't the core issue. He simply wasn't in a position to be vocal or physical; not wide out in the open.

But if she wanted it.

If she *had* to know ...

Here it was.

Vaslav only broke their kiss once he'd licked

practically every drop of pigment of her lipstick from her mouth, and he finished it off by wiping away what smudge remained on her right upper lip. She vibrated under his touch, her words a whisper along his thumb before he could pull it away when she said, "You didn't have to get in your feelings about it. I only said it so you could know I wanted you to kiss me, too."

A laugh creeped its way out, but it was too light and easy to be dark. It even shocked him as he scrubbed a palm over his own mouth to wipe away what stains might be there. "Calling me any name but my own is either a challenge or a slight, and both will be enough to provoke a response, *kisska.*"

She sucked in another one of those shaky breaths.

Vaslav would have told Vera right then and there that she was in for a world of trouble with him if she kept on pushing him like she did, but the clock struck ten.

And the tower started to sparkle.

Or rather, the lights did. Every hour on the hour, the Eiffel Tower's lights would sparkle for five minutes. He hadn't even had the chance to admire the way she licked her swollen lips for another taste of his kiss when his head snapped up at the flashing lights.

He'd never had the issue before—lights triggered his migraine pain sometimes, yes, but not that sudden stiffness in his neck and confusion muddling his mind. It was almost like his vision started to quake, and with it came a burst of scattered pain that started in the base of his skull. It was the overwhelming pressure that made his temples feel like they might explode that accompanied a heavy weight swaying Vaslav's shoulders, making his loss of control all the more apparent.

It happened faster than that day at The Swan House. He couldn't slink away to hide what was quickly coming on.

You're having seizures, he remembered the doctor explaining to him that night, opting after to call it simply a neurological event when he realized Vaslav wasn't open to labeling a terrifying, new symptom he'd been trying to keep hidden.

"*Vas!*" he heard Vera yell.

"*No hospitals*," he grunted, the Russian sharp and bitter on his tongue.

Or maybe that bitterness was blood.

When did he hit the ground?

22.

"Oh, my God, Vas—*somebody help me!*"

Vera screamed the words, and no sooner did they pass her lips than a man kneeled beside her.

"Here, I'll help you get him up on his side," the man grunted in heavily accented English as he placed his hands to Vas's trembling lower back. "My oldest son has epilepsy. He's a tall guy, too, and sometimes you just need an extra pair of hands. Shit, did he bite his tongue?"

Vera, too shocked to do anything let alone talk or reply to the kind tone of the friendly man, helped him roll a shaking Vaslav to his side. The seizure looked a lot like the one that had happened in the gallery— between Vas's wild, rolling eyes and his unstoppable trembling, she thought he still managed to maintain some sense of awareness. But not any control.

She noticed the tiny trickle of blood that fell from the corner of Vaslav's mouth, mixed in with his saliva.

"It's not too bad." Noticing her silence and fast

breaths, the blond man who had stepped into help asked, "Does this happen often?"

God.

She didn't know.

She opted to say something that didn't feel like a lie. "It's happened before."

The man nodded. "As long as it doesn't last longer than two minutes, and he starts to gain some awareness, we won't have to call for emergency services. Okay?"

Vera, now fighting through hiccups and the shame of a tear-streaked face while a small crowd gathered, only nodded back in reply. She fought hiccups to hide her rising sobs. It all happened so fast. From his kiss to the lights, and she saw the dazed look in Vaslav's eyes just before he squinted back in pain and started to sway. She had fallen with him, trying to catch a brick wall of a man, and the throbbing ache in her bad ankle let her know which leg had taken the brunt of the impact.

"I'm Natan," the man said.

"Vera, oh God! What happened?"

Hannah.

Vera was still trying to process the last minute— and a half?—and in that time, forgot about her friend. Wasn't that just her luck?

Hannah was quick to grab Vera's clutch that had fallen a few feet away, and dropped beside her, asking only, "Can I help?"

Vaslav's trembling has become a lot less intense, and focused mostly on the end of his limbs and a bit in his neck. But at the same time, his once open eyes were now squeezed tightly shut, and his teeth clenched so hard she could hear them grinding.

"No, I think he's coming out of it, actually. Could someone call a cab?" Natan asked no one in particular. "I'm sure he'll want to go home once he's up on his feet. You know where he's going?"

At that question, Vera nodded. "Yeah, we're staying together. Not far from here."

She rattled off the address, even though nobody asked.

"Your friend?" she heard Hannah ask.

"Yeah, I guess he was out for a walk."

She didn't look at Hannah when she lied.

"Vas?" Vera asked, whispering his name a second time while she drifted her hands over his side to offer him any comfort.

If he knew she was there, would it help?

There were too many questions, and too much happening all at once. Someone in the crowd made a statement in French that was translated by Natan.

"They called a car service," he said.

She didn't ask which one.

Who cared?

Vaslav was trying to talk, and though his words were stuttered and forced through his closed teeth, she heard what he tried to say, and understood him perfectly well.

"*G-get me—g-go.*"

"We're going to get you up as soon as you feel like you can," Vera told him, ignoring the worried, but curious, gaze of her friend who had kneeled on her other side.

"He's okay, right?" Hannah asked.

That time, she did lie. "Yeah, he'll be fine."

The truth?

Well, Vera didn't have a clue.

*

"Call me tomorrow, okay? We have to at least do breakfast before you fly out," Hannah insisted, holding tight to Vera's hand on the sidewalk.

It was the only thing keeping her in place when every inch of her screamed to get in the waiting Uber. Her attention wavered between the man hiding his face in his hands, sitting in the back of the blue SUV, and the lights of the tower behind Hannah.

"If I can," Vera replied.

That seemed to be enough for her friend. Hannah let go of Vera's hand, and stepped back, finally letting her climb in the back of the car that had been called by an onlooker earlier. As she closed the door, and waved goodbye to Hannah, she was grateful that she'd gotten the chance to thank the man who'd first stepped in to help.

Especially after Vaslav had been worse than just mean to the guy when he'd finally felt good enough to stand. Even going as far as ripping the good Samaritan's hands off him when Natan had only been trying to help keep Vas steady as they walked to the waiting car. He'd cussed at the man, too, when Natan apologized.

Nothing Vera tried to do calmed Vaslav down until he was hidden in the SUV, away from any onlookers. He crouched at the far door, rocking a bit where he was balled against the seat with his face still tucked into his open palms.

"*Madame?*"

The man at the front of the vehicle, behind the wheel, glanced at Vera in the rearview mirror as she scooted to the middle of the bench seat to be closer to a closed off Vas. The driver repeated the question she hadn't heard the first time.

The address.

Vera rattled it off, and figured it was enough for the driver because he pulled out onto the street without another word. She didn't turn around to see them leave her friend and the tower behind; instead, she scooted even closer to Vas. He hadn't said more than a handful of words since they got him back on his feet, but his low groans now concerned Vera. Especially when he started massaging his hands rougher into his face like he was trying to relieve pressure.

"Are you okay? Can I help?"

She reached for him, but Vas jerked away.

"Just get me back to the apartment," he snapped, the words muffled by his hands. Yet, not enough to hide the bite.

He was clearly in pain.

"Come here," Vera said, refusing to be put off by his harsh demeanor. She reached for him again, this time grabbing him by his wrists and tugging to pull him toward her. That was all it took, and he practically sunk into her lap, his face buried into her clothes.

He didn't take his hands away from his face, and his groaning turned into a steady stream of cusses that varied between English and Russian.

Out of all his grumbled and hissed anger, she heard one thing clearly.

"Worst fucking time for this shit."

How often did this happen?

"What happened back there?" she asked him.

Quietly, so the man behind the wheel didn't hear.
Vaslav didn't answer.

"We're almost there."

He didn't act like he heard that, either.

*

Vera blinked, too exhausted to read the time right
the first time on her watch. Partly because the glass
face had been broken sometime over the night.
Maybe when she hit the ground?

Her ankle still ached, too.

Not as much, though.

The fact it was nearly half past twelve in the
morning should have been a clue to her that she
desperately needed to get some sleep. Especially as
she'd been up before the sun even rose to get ready
for her day with Hannah.

Still, Vera didn't move.

Sitting with her back against the closed bathroom
door, she couldn't even get lost in the sound of her
own thoughts with the noise of water rushing so
loudly in the room. Apparently, the master suite's
shower stall was equipped with powerful, positionable
showerheads at nearly every angle.

Vas hadn't cared what one she managed to get
turned on for him—which was good, because she had
no clue how to run the damn panel on the side of the
wall, tiled in the same grey, black, and white as the
shower.

He asked for two things.

Hot water, and darkness.

Vera made it happen in the master bath, but then
she couldn't bear to leave after Vaslav stumbled into

the fairly large shower stall. Once she turned the light off, and the hot steam started to fill the room, she realized how quiet Vas was.

If she headed to her bedroom down the hall, she might not hear him if he needed help again. Not that she thought he would appreciate her pointing it out. So, instead she sat on the floor, against the opened door, and wasn't even sure if Vas knew she was there.

In her struggle to get only a few of the dozen shower heads working, she'd soaked her jeans, leaving her in a pair of panties and an oversized T-shirt she found tossed at the end of the bed in the attached bedroom.

At some point, her ringing phone almost pulled her away from the bathroom, but her concern for Vas won out. He told her *nothing*.

He offered no explanation once they arrived back at the apartment; and even when she outright demanded he at least tell her if he should go to a twenty-four-hour emergency room just to be checked out, he simply looked her dead in her face with nothing but a scowl, and then uttered, "Don't do that."

What was she supposed to do?

"*Vera!*"

The guttural shout of her name sent Vera scrambling off the floor toward the direction that it came. Inside the shower's stall. She had to step over his pile of sopping wet clothes that he'd thrown out at some point, and the darkness made it hard for her to see the ledge stepping up into the shower.

She nearly tripped on it.

The only light inside the shower came from the waterproof, digital wall panel controlled by touch.

The screen apparently didn't sleep, but he didn't complain about the glow. He'd damn near roared about shutting off the overhead lights, though.

At the far end of the five-foot long shower stall that was wide enough for two people to stand comfortable side by side, Vaslav sat with his back against the tiles on a bench made of bamboo that had been built into the wall. Just out of full reach of the steady sprays of water from the heads in the shower's middle. With one foot tucked under the bench a bit and his other leg out straight, a hand towel, soaked with water, was all that offered him privacy.

Vera hesitated just inside the stall, before the spray of water.

He stared up at her, gaze open and clear. At least, there was that. His one eye remained tightly shut, making his already expressive eyebrows even more severe as he watched her.

"You need something?" she asked.

He was in pain; she understood that, now. He was still one hell of a sight there. A fit, tall body made of defined muscles covered in various tattoos. From stars on his knees, to onion domed spires on his chest. Despite being covered to an extent, the wet towel did extraordinarily little to hide the outline of his flaccid penis, and when she averted her eyes a bit higher, it was only to land on the dark dusting of hair that trailed up his toned stomach to his navel.

How could she not look?

She had never even seen the man in anything less than slacks and a dress shirt; not that he was concerned with her staring.

Vaslav barely gave her time to appreciate the sight of him, anyway. "Come here—do that thing again."

"What?"

"In the car," he told her. "It helped with your fingers. Come here and *do that*."

She stiffened on the spot at the way he hissed the final words at her. If someone else spoke to her like that, with enough venom to burn on contact, she would have walked away; it was only because she didn't think he even understood the way he sounded when he was in pain that stopped her from doing exactly that—leaving him there.

It helped to be touched.

That's what he didn't want to say. Because the only thing Vera had done in the ride to the apartment was stroke his scalp while his head was in her lap.

She couldn't refuse him at all when he let out a hard breath and said, "Please."

The temperature of the hot water only stung Vera for a few seconds before she could stand it, and by the time she was kneeling on the floor between Vaslav's opened legs reaching for his face, she was fine.

Soaked again, but fine.

"Could we at least call Igor?"

"It's just migraines," he told her quietly as she dragged her manicured nails through the wet strands of his hair, and he turned his scarred cheek to face her while he stared at the shower wall.

Vera's hands stilled, and while she tried to meet his gaze, he outright avoided hers. She couldn't help but think he wasn't telling her the truth. Those who had nothing to hide, hid nothing. Wasn't that how the saying went?

"Or is it more than just migraines? I mean, this is twice I've seen you have a—"

Without warning, the side of his fisted hand slammed down to the bamboo bench. The action stopped her prodding, but as if he'd done nothing at all, Vaslav said, "It used to be just migraines."

"So, what is it *now*?"

Vaslav swallowed hard, but she realized his problem before he even admitted it. "I don't really know."

23.

"Just tell me where it is."

"I'll get it, I said," Vas hissed back to Vera in reply.

She stood firm in the open doorway of the master bathroom, unmoved by his returning attitude or that his tone suggested he was quickly getting angry as well. "Vas, the longer you sit there and argue with me about where the damn bag is and who is going to get it, well … that's all we're going to sit here and do. Just tell me."

He didn't want her in his things; nothing personal, he was just anal about that sort of issue. Call it his nature after years of having cell searches and no real possessions but what he could keep taped to cement walls.

"Vera—"

"Vas, it's almost two in the morning. *Where is the bag?*"

"There's a hidden pocket at the bottom of the luggage. It's inside the larger pocket."

Fuck it, he thought.

"The bag is long and thin; it sits between the bars for the wheels."

"Anything else?" she asked, sighing a little.

He wished he could stand to lift his head and stare at Vera for longer than two or three seconds at a time, but the dimly lit hallway was still more than enough light to make him want to stab his eyeballs out. He probably wouldn't even feel the knife going in considering the pain behind his eye sockets could only be described as stabbing.

"You're gonna have to cut some wrapping off," he muttered.

There might be a mix of pepper and other nasally irritating spices wrapped within the cellophane that were known to confuse and deter sniffer dogs in airports, but he wasn't going to offer that information to Vera. She would figure it out herself and fill in the whys without him admitting any guilt, when she found his pills—and other medications—where he'd hidden the bag to smuggle it into France.

A stack of passports, Vas had.

Matching prescriptions for narcotics, and other medications he was supposed to take but sometimes didn't depending on his mood, for the names on said passports was another matter.

Vera hesitated in the doorway, turning only a bit as she asked, "What happens if they find it during customs check or something?"

"If they find what?" he returned, arching one tense eyebrow.

"Never mind."

He dropped his gaze as her footsteps padded away from the bathroom and deeper into the bedroom.

Although she had done her best to be quiet while he'd been in the shower, this was the most silence he'd had since getting back to the apartment. He could almost stand to leave his eyelids half open for more than a handful of seconds at a time. Puke didn't churn in his stomach while the pain refused to cease.

All in all, the migraine had leveled out to mostly the pressure and stabbing behind his eye sockets, and an otherwise unshakeable tiredness in the rest of his limbs. Actually, he partly blamed that on the earlier seizure. It would be mostly gone by morning—the migraine, that was; the other bit ...

Well, maybe it was time to make a call.

As he listened to Vera rifle through the items in his one piece of luggage to find the pocket inside the pocket at the bottom, Vaslav readjusted his seat on the tiled steps leading up to the deep jacuzzi tub. At least, he'd found a larger towel to wrap around his waist because it offered a bit of warmth in the cold air of the bathroom, but nudity was really the least of his concerns.

What *was* dignity?

He'd lost that a long time ago.

When footsteps carried outside the bedroom, Vaslav figured Vera must have found his hidden bag. She'd need scissors to get the significant layer of cellophane off, so he undoubtedly had a few more minutes alone.

Part of him liked that.

Another part wanted her to come back.

Vaslav did his best to ignore the part of his brain that was all man—entirely human. He preferred when he just existed, when he just *was*. It was easier to be the person he had to be who did what he had to do when he didn't attach too much of himself to anything or anyone. Being reminded that he was nothing more than a man at the end of the day, who enjoyed a certain woman's company, and the way she helped to get him through the worst of a bad night, was not high on his list of priorities.

Too bad his fucking brain didn't want to listen and follow along with what should be the plan.

Or his cock, for that matter.

Irony truly was a bitch.

It should be cruel how his cock could stay semi-hard if Vera was within reaching distance of his hands—and certainly if he could *see* her—when he couldn't even get his dick to twitch if there was a prospect of pain on the horizon. Unless it came to her, apparently.

Or her *touch*.

On the fourth of six steps leading into the tub, Vaslav had a decent amount of room to stretch out his legs as he leaned back. Massaging his fingers into his eyes did little to give him relief; he found more when his thoughts drifted back to the way Vera's fingernails had glided over his wet scalp, scratching lightly enough to make the fine hair on his body stand on end. Thinking about that led into the way she'd traced the three tattooed spires on his chest, placed between the thieves cross he had done under his throat, and the Cyrillic spelling of his family name along his lower stomach. The name had been a prison job he was never fond of due to shaky lines and shitty ink.

Once on, though, a *vor's* tattoos were there. He didn't believe in do overs when it came to the tattoos he'd earned—from the eight-pointed stars under his clavicles to the captain's epaulettes on his shoulders. Some of his tattoos had faded, having been done when he was young, and he never even bothered to have a fill in for color after the whites and pinks on his spires practically disappeared. The only way one of his tattoos would change, was if they were burned off.

And there was no man powerful enough to order it done. Not while he sat in the seat he did, anyway.

"Is that okay—like that, I mean?" Vera had asked him, always willing to meet his gaze when she was touching his body, but never for too long.

She had asked the question again when she moved onto the crown, a newer piece added into the thieves' cross, in the middle portion of his chest. She got the same answer then, too.

His silence.

If he didn't like it, Vas would have told her so. Immediately.

The problem was, he liked it too much.

She had the hands of a goddamn angel—it took him no time at all to figure that out. Delicate, but strong fingers that worked softly into aching muscles in his arms, thighs, and calves that he didn't even realize he had until she worked the knots out. She spent extra time on each of his tattooed fingers. Her touch stayed steady and slow on the skull, black oval, tiny crown, and even the first initial of his family's name tattooed on his left hand. The number—the year of his birth—on his right hand was probably easier for her to understand.

He couldn't have told her to stop even if he had wanted to, but the woman had been intent on staying in that shower with him until he told her to leave.

Vas couldn't form the words.

It'd been a long time since something felt good. Especially when he was in pain.

"Is this what you need?"

The question sent Vaslav sitting up straight on the steps again to find Vera had come back to the bathroom without him even hearing her footsteps. Outstretched in her hand where he could see, she showed off a small, thin plastic latch box. One shake of her hand, and the pills inside rattled.

"Well," he settled on saying, the gruffness of his tone belying the fact he still had a lot of pain behind his eyes, "there'll be something in there, anyway. Bring it to me, *kisska*. Leave the lights off."

She did, not reaching for the switch on the wall and instead popping open the little latch box as she crossed the large bathroom. "There's just a bunch of pills in here, how do you know which is which?"

"Depends on what I want to do, doesn't it?"

Vera gave him a look as she extended the box to his outstretched hand once she was close enough. At least, she'd changed her wet, oversized t-shirt into a new, dry one.

"Who does that belong to?" he asked her, not bothering to pay attention to the box of pills that could put a serious dent in the scale of his pain depending on which he took.

Or rather, they could make the time pass easier.

"What?" Vera asked.

"That shirt you're wearing. And the other one."

"I just … I don't know, I found them and threw them on. I didn't want to bother wasting time looking for—"

"It's not yours?"

Vera cocked her head to the side a bit, saying,

"No."

And the shirt wasn't *his*.

"Go change," he muttered. "Into something *you* recognize."

"Excuse me?"

Vaslav ignored her tone, tipping the box over into his palm to eye the rainbow of pills that fell out. "Do you know how many medications I've been on over the last fifteen years of my life?"

Vera didn't reply.

She also didn't move to change.

"Too many," he muttered. "Every kind they've come out with for migraines. Nothing worked. I have access to every pharmaceutical narcotic I could want, but they never really help. Nothing blocks the pain to the brain; what shuts that off? Oh, that's before all the various antipsychotics—you might as well be a fucking *slug* on those. And then it's just a cocktail, see? Of side effects, different dosages, and bullshit. All of it is just bullshit."

Because none of it had worked.

The woman standing only a couple of feet away cleared her throat. "If you're mixing them incorrectly, maybe. I could see how—"

"I got tired of being a guinea pig for a doctor who doesn't know the way the inside of my head feels seven days a fucking week," Vas barked, quieting Vera instantly.

"I'm sorry."

"For what?"

He glared hard at her.

Vera at least had the nerve to stare back. "That you hurt. That it doesn't get better. I guess that's the only thing that worked out for me after my accident. The pain got better; or I learned to manage it until it did, anyway."

Vaslav let out a low, steady exhale before he dropped a few pills back into the container and opted for the one that wouldn't knock him out. He *would* get a little bit of that euphoria to take the edge off, though.

"Bottoms up," he told her.

Vera didn't blink a lash when he popped back, and swallowed, a Vicodin dry.

"Shouldn't you be taking something else?" she asked. "Or do you?"

"Like what?"

"Any kind of seizure meds, or something?"

"Why haven't you changed yet?" he asked instead of answering. At least, the hem of the oversized shirt stopped at her mid-thigh. As she put a hand on her hip, he was given just a peek at the simple white cotton panties she had on underneath.

Vera's gaze narrowed. "I'll change when I go to bed."

"You'll change right now, or I'll cut the damn thing off."

She blinked, her pretty pout falling open at his threat.

Was she listening now?

He sure hoped so.

Vas only smirked. "*Spasibo, kisska.* Hurry."

"Go to hell."

That earned her a scoff as he rested his back to the steps once more and covered his eyes with an arm while the pill settled into his gut. "Oh, Vera … haven't you figured it out yet? I'm already *there*."

"You're a real asshole. You know that?"

"Yes, actually, I do. That also changes nothing, including that fucking shirt on your body. Get it *off*."

Vera let out a sound of indignation. "It's just a shirt!"

"Not my shirt—not yours, either. Probably someone's … like the man who lives here. I already dislike him enough; he really doesn't need a reason for me to kill him."

All at once, the bathroom went quiet.

She didn't even breathe.

"I will cut off," he murmured under his breath. "If you want to go down that route."

He swore he heard her swallow.

"You barely even kissed me. Now you're worried about whose clothes I might be wearing?"

"Barely, Vera?"

"Well—"

"Barely?"

Because he remembered that differently.

"Fine," she grumbled, her heels squeaking as she turned on the spot. "I'll go change."

"Bring back vodka from the bar in the kitchen!"

"You don't need to drink!"

"Woman, I didn't ask you what I goddamn well needed," he shouted back.

Too late, though.

Vera was already gone.

He let it slide.

Mostly because he was trying to ignore the fact that his dick was hard again. Maybe he could drink that problem away.

Right, he thought. *Good fucking luck.*

Why did she have to be sassy?

Vaslav always liked a combative woman.

They gave the best lays.

*

By the time Vera returned to the bedroom, Vaslav had left the bathroom and found a more comfortable seat in the corner of the master bedroom. He'd hated the space the moment he walked into it—all bright white with tall, painted pillory at each four corners of the bed. Even the cushions on the bed, with the head of it facing large windows that could be opened to view the street and tower in the distance, were a crisp, fluffy white.

Pierre Aubert clearly liked the color. The entire apartment was designed with white or yellow as focus tones for the major spaces.

Vaslav would rather burn the place to the ground.

The only good thing about the room was the size, the fact it had an attached bathroom, and the heavy drapes framing each window that could block out all light once shut. But with the sky dark outside, he didn't want the curtains closed.

What would be the point?

"Any better?" Vera asked.

Massaging his thumb firmly into his left temple, he didn't even open his eyes to watch her enter the space. Instead, he'd listened to the soft pat-pat of her footsteps leading her across the hardwood floor to where he sat in the leather bucket chair.

"No," he replied simply.

His eyes popped open at the glass *clink* that echoed. He almost smiled at the item she had sat on the circular, wooden side table next to his chair.

"Still don't think you need anything to drink," she

muttered, glowering at the half filled forty-ounce bottle of top shelf vodka. At least the Frenchman kept good liquor on hand. "Are you even supposed to mix whatever you took with alcohol?"

"It was a Vicodin."

She glanced his way, meeting his narrowed gaze. "*So?*"

"Never hurt before."

His clipped response must not have been what she was expecting—or wanting—because Vera only scoffed, and shook her head before turning to leave. "Fine, keep your vodka and pills. I'm going to bed. You don't need anything else, right?"

Vas reached out and snatched her wrist in his grasp before she could go anywhere. The action had her spinning back around before he'd even blinked up at her again, and though she tugged to pull away, he refused to let go.

"What now?" she asked.

He wished that wetness in her eyes didn't bother him so much. Or even the frown tugging down at her tempting mouth. It was even more cumbersome to him because he had a good idea that he was the cause for her displeasure.

Shocker.

He usually was the source of discontent in the lives of people around him.

"The robe is much better," he murmured.

Vera's throat flexed with a swallow, but otherwise, she didn't acknowledge the fact she'd changed out of the unknown t-shirt for a silk robe she cinched with a loose knot in the middle.

She tugged on her wrist once more.

He still held firm.

"Why won't you let me go? God. You act like you can't stand to have me in the same room, Vas. Give me some time to breathe, okay?"

He chuckled, as dry as it was. "I'm in pain."

"So, what, that justifies your—"

He yanked firmly enough on her wrist, when she wasn't expecting it, that Vera practically stumbled over her feet, almost right into his lap.

Her hands sprawled to his knees and skirted up his thighs to catch herself, those big blue eyes of hers locking onto his when she looked up with a sharp gasp. He didn't give her time to respond or understand why he'd done what he'd done; instead, he leaned close and caught her upturned face in the palms of his hands.

Softly, he stole a featherlight kiss.

Then, Vas let her go.

"Goodnight," he said.

Vera didn't move, but he could feel the soft tremor working its way through her fingertips that dug into his upper thighs through the towel still wrapped around his waist. "You could just … ask for a kiss."

"Could I?"

She blinked, her stare dropping to his mouth. "Well—"

"Or do you like it when I take it from you more, *kisska*?"

"I don't like when you give me whiplash."

Vas cocked his head sideways, drinking in the sight of her kneeled down between his open legs in a thin, flimsy robe that had managed to open just enough for him to see what she wasn't wearing. The cotton panties stayed on, though.

"Vera," he murmured.

"Yes?"

"I'd have fucked you tonight. If you would have asked me under the tower, I would have made sure you could still see the crowd when I fucked you bent over the closest thing I could find. And here you are, concerned about my mood when I'm just in pain. Do you understand how silly I think that is?"

Those long, dark lashes of hers swept downward. She even nibbled a bit on her bottom lip, and that was enough to get his cock thickening where it had been resting against his inner thigh.

"It's not silly to me," she returned.

So be it.

"Go to bed," he told her.

She still didn't move.

Heat traveled down his gut, dropping lower into his balls when her hand shifted a bit on his upper thigh. She didn't look down to see the outline of his erection growing under the towel, but could she feel it?

Did she sense it?

"I could stay," Vera whispered after seconds ticked by and neither of them moved an inch. "I helped earlier when you were in the shower. I don't mind doing that again if you—"

"I don't want pity."

"Why would I pity you?"

Why wouldn't she?

Maybe it was his own foolish pride that kept him from saying the words he wanted to: *yes, please stay.* Vaslav wasn't accustomed to something like shame— a lot of that had been stripped from him in prison, but he felt it, then. A deep sense of humiliation at the fact he so desperately wanted this woman to crawl into bed with him, stroke him to sleep with those soft hands of hers, and let him use her like he believed she would.

He *wanted* that.

More than anything.

Except he couldn't make himself say it.

"Go to bed," he ordered one last time.

Let me drown myself in vodka, beautiful girl.

Vera lingered only a second longer. Long enough to meet his gaze one more time, and find a blank coldness staring back. He said nothing as she stood, fixed her robe with a bit of pink color flushing her cheeks, and then turned to leave.

At the doorway, she stopped again.

"What?" he asked in a whooshed exhale.

The dull pain flared in the base of his skull again. If she noticed his sudden scowl from the pain, or if she took it for her, he didn't know. She had a knack for seeing the shit he was typically good at hiding from others, though. Who could say?

"You never said what would happen if I asked *you*," she said.

"Asked me for what?"

"For you. If I asked for you."

"To fuck you?"

Vera lifted one shoulder. "You never said."

"Vera—"

"Yeah, yeah. *Go to bed.*"

She even had his tone down in her mockery.

He might have laughed.

But then she said, "I wanted you to. I still want you to, Vas."

God knew he should have made her go to bed. This would go nowhere good, very damn fast.

Instead, he replied only, "Crawl to me—and take off the robe."

Vera stiffened a bit, her chin lifting subtly. "Excuse me?"

"I will call another woman to do far worse—in fact, she already has. Where's my phone?"

Another sharp suck of air echoed from the woman in the doorway. "You … *prick*."

That barely even stung.

She didn't even say it like she meant it.

"If you want me, you'll crawl for it. Like a kitten coming for a stroke, Vera. Down on all fours, in nothing but white cotton, and you'll even ask me *nicely*. Again, if you want it."

He expected another one of her curses. Hell, if she ever spoke to him again after this trip, he'd be shocked. But if the woman was going to play his games, then she would do so by his rules.

Including this.

Vera's tongue peeked out to wet the seam of her plush bottom lip. "Why?"

"It turns me on."

Another wash of pink colored her cheeks, and she dropped his stare once more. It told him everything he needed to know about this woman and just how much she could tempt him without even having to try.

"And I would dare say," he added, "that it turns you on, too, *kisska*. Deny it."

She didn't say a word.

She also didn't need to.

Not when she dropped the robe from one naked shoulder. He grinned when the second one followed, and she lifted her head for him to see her face once more.

"All the way to the floor," Vas told her.

She let the silk fall.

24.

Vera's skin pebbled exposed to nothing but air, and when Vaslav's gaze turned away from her to the bottle she'd left on the table, she almost covered her bare breasts with her arms. Resisting the urge was easier said than done when insecurity creeped in to whisper *why doesn't he want to look at you?*

Except he did keep watching her. Out of the corner of his eye, while he unscrewed the top off the vodka, that steely gaze of his raked her up and down. Vera felt every inch, swell, and curve of her body that he lingered on.

For years, her body had been on display as a ballerina—just as much as her technique and style was when she danced. Behind the scenes, there was always a handful of people at the ready with measuring tape, or a strict dietary plan, and some comment about whatever invisible fat they found on her already stick-thin body.

At the same time, she received unending praise,

adoration, and love when she was on the stage. Talk about a fucking complex.

If anything, she had learned to be unashamed about her body. That she was beautiful, whether she was fifteen pounds under weight so she could jump higher, or twenty pounds heavier than she'd been the last time she had been on a stage.

"Your career has been beneficial to what's standing in front of me, no?"

"Being forced to quit did, actually," she returned. "And running."

Vas chuckled, leaning back to settle into the bucket chair with the open bottle of vodka balancing on his thigh. He palmed the top, cocking his head to the side a bit as he took her in again. "Right, you're a runner."

She felt the shiver crawl up her spine at the way he called her that—like it might not be a good thing, even though his husky drawl did the most wicked things to her insides.

"Can't forget that," he added. "Are you still going to crawl, my sweet little kitten?"

It was the sardonic way he twisted the question out that sent her blush blooming. With no robe to hide her chest, he could even see the way it flushed down to the valley between her small breasts.

"*Derr'mo*," he swore. "That's a lovely sight."

"Yes," she told him, "I'll still crawl."

Because he didn't think she would. It was obvious to her that Vaslav liked to rise to a challenge, and he expected the same from those around him. Even making her crawl across the floor like a kitten who wanted him to stroke her between the ears—he thought she wouldn't do it, and if his respect came from proving him wrong, so be it.

The second Vera's palms touched the hardwood floor, she understood entirely that she had given Vaslav an immense amount of control. To make a woman crawl across the floor and ask for him, well, that would be humiliating enough for anyone to refuse.

Except that was part of what she liked about it.

That, and the way he tipped the top of the vodka bottle up to take a swig. A few gulps, actually, before he set it back down. All the while, he'd never taken his eyes off her. Or the way her shoulders and hips bobbed and swayed as she inched forward.

"How have men touched you?" he asked.

Vera hesitated just long enough to decide to push up where she could kneel on her bent legs. Folding her hands in her lap, she asked, "You threatened to cut a shirt off me earlier because it might belong to someone else—now you're asking about other men touching me?"

"*Net.*" He smiled, or the closest thing to it, before pulling the bottle to his lips for another long pull of liquor. "I asked a very careful question, and I expect a very careful answer."

"Most, all, or specific?"

Vas shrugged. "Like I said, a careful answer."

Right.

"Like glass. They treated me like fine china."

He pointed a finger at her while he discarded the vodka bottle to the side table. "Ah, priceless and fragile."

"And I only get taken out and played with when it's convenient, or someone's throwing a party. Boring doesn't excite me."

That earned her one of his dark laughs. She loved

229

the way his genuine amusement could soften his severe features ever so slightly, not that she would ever dare to tell him that. She got the impression that this man didn't laugh very much.

"A fucking shame, that," he murmured, his grin fading while his tongue swept the line of his lower lip. "Who told you to stop? Here, kitty-kitty."

She pressed her lips together to keep from laughing, instead mumbling a weak, "Fuck you."

Vas winked. "Well, isn't that the point?"

It was.

And she planned to see it through.

Her fingertips barely touched the floor again when he asked, "All, or most?"

"Do you want to talk, or me to crawl?"

Vas clicked his tongue, considering that for a moment before he said simply, "I am sure you can do both, *kisska.*"

She moved forward, closing a foot of the ten that was left between them. Only the dimly lit streets and the glow of the moon in the dark sky filtering in from the open shades offered any light. The lighting from the hallway did nothing but halo the door behind her.

"Most," she said.

"And a few have been?"

"Very good teachers."

The hint of a smile curved the edge of his lips, and as he nodded like he was satisfied with the extent of his careful prodding about her prior sexual experience, he reached for the bottle again. By the time he had gulped down a good inch of the liquor, she'd nearly finished closing the distance to his chair.

At his feet, she kneeled again, using her legs to rest on and keeping her hands in her lap, like she had done in the middle of the floor.

Vaslav watched her.

Seconds ticked slowly by.

"Did they treat you that way, maybe, because of who you are?" he asked, then. "Because they were not the kind of men who could afford to treat you otherwise?"

Vera shrugged, all too aware of his stare drawing a hot path down her chest, over her breasts, and then lower to the waistband of her plain white cotton panties. "I thought we were done with careful questions?"

Vas lifted his brow. "Did I ever say we were?"

"You didn't say we *weren't*."

"*Vera*—"

She let out a sigh, glancing away from him to the window where the shades were wide open. She couldn't see the tower in the distance—the lights had finally been shut off for the evening, and she wouldn't see it lit up again because tomorrow, they'd be gone.

"Probably because of my father," she admitted. "Almost everyone I've dated publicly has been vetted or warned or threatened—or some various combination—and I've not found a nice guy yet that knows what to do when a woman climbs on top and tells him to choke her and call her a slut, you know?"

"Nice guys have morals, Vera."

She heard what he didn't say.

I'm not one of those.

His finger, tapping a beat to the top of the sidewall of the bucket chair, stopped, and the lack of noise drew her attention his way once more. It came as a surprise to her to find him still watching her.

"And what's a little degradation between friends,

hmm?" he asked.

Vera lifted a bit higher, then, enough that she could reach for his thighs still covered by the towel wrapped around his waist. She felt the way those firm, solid muscles in his strong thighs clenched when her fingernails dug in harder.

She wanted a good grip, that's all.

With her breasts grazing his bare knees, and her chin tilted up so when he looked down, their faces lined up, she wondered what he saw there. Did he like that she was willing to get on her knees? That she could be sweet and submit; that she could pretend as if her thumb weren't resting along the ridge of his erection outlined under the towel?

"Is that what we are, Vas? Friends?"

"We're certainly not lovers."

She pulled back from him, just enough to draw her steady, slow hands lower on his muscular thighs. "*Not yet.*"

He dragged in a breath, and she heard the way it caught once in his throat. "Right, not yet. Did you figure out why I wanted you to crawl?"

Of course, she did.

The second he said it.

"You wanted me on my knees."

"I do like the view," he returned just as easily, flooding her gut with heat from his domineering attention. "How long will you suck me?"

"Until you're dry and then until you're clean."

"You better. Find your cream, *kisska*. And make sure you lap up every damn drop. Like a good kitten would do."

"You're still an asshole."

Vas let his head fall back to the wall of the chair so

he could stare up at the ceiling when he replied, "But I bet you like that, too."

He wasn't wrong.

She just wouldn't say so. Everybody had their pride.

"Come on," he said, that husky desire coming back in a blink as he folded veiny, muscular arms behind his head, so he had a nice, propped view. "I want to see you swallow me, Vera."

25.

He knew she'd look heaven-sent on her knees in front of him. The very picture of temptation between his widened legs as she peeled open the towel around his waist. Vaslav offered her no help; he didn't so much as shift upward to help loosen the towel. If this was what she was set on doing, then she could do it herself.

Besides, he *was* enjoying the view.

Vaslav only looked away when Vera finally had his cock—hard enough to throb within her tight palms— free. It was as good as he expected it to be—how she needed both hands, one on top of the other and used both to stroke all nine and a half thick inches of him. Air rushed up from his lungs the second she squeezed delicate fingers around his shaft, but he swallowed it back with a gulp of vodka from the bottle he already had waiting in his hand.

"Now?" he heard her ask when he put the bottle back.

Did this woman know she was perfect? That she knew to wait without him telling her; that she tested him in all the right ways, like simply asking if she could continue.

"*Net*," came his low reply.

Russian was easier; it slipped from his mind before the longer, more descriptive direction he'd wanted to give. He didn't think Vera would appreciate being told he would consider cutting her hands off at the wrists if she removed them from his cock at that moment. Even the sway of her shoulders as she double stroked him was mesmerizing.

With a grip that became firmer as she came up on his shaft in the best way, she kept a steady pace and watched him through lowered lashes all the while. It was the pleased, teasing smile playing on her lips that told him she saw through his carefully crafted facade.

The bottle he used as a distraction.

The almost disinterested expression.

Even the steady exhales lifting his chest.

She stared at his eyes, like she could see right through him, and that's where she found the truth. That every stroke of her hands put him a little closer to snapping; that it felt almost too fucking good to breathe.

Control was Vaslav's *favorite* thing. An unspoken expectation in every aspect of his life. He had no other choice than to be this way because when he was stripped of his control … It was the one thing that once lost, so was he—entirely *gone*.

He should be concerned with the way the Vicodin was already churning badly with the vodka in his gut, but because all the blood in his fucking brain had gone straight to his cock, well … did it *really* matter?

"Come here," he demanded, adding only in a grunt, "Closer, Vera."

Her rhythm working his cock was unsteady as she lifted to tilt her head into his opened, offered palm. He caught her under her throat, yanking her up for a vicious kiss that didn't even allow her to breathe between his tongue cutting past her parting lips. He wanted one more taste of her, and as he shoved her back to her knees without ever taking his hand away from the underside of her jaw, he could still see where the roughness of his beard had left her soft mouth a little red.

"Now can I?" she asked again, adding the whispered, "*Please?*"

His hand shifted just enough that his thumb could stroke over her lips, and she sucked the tip of the digit inside a teasing cocoon of wetness and heat. Withdrawing his thumb from her mouth to leave her bottom lip glossy when he traced it again, his hand then slipped around to tangle in the hair at the nape of her neck. She whimpered when he fisted the strands, but then let out a breathless laugh.

"Now," she said.

"*Now*," he agreed.

He pulled her down, the strands of hair he hadn't caught in his fist pooling in his lap like the kiss of a soft feather while the silken warmth of her mouth engulfed the head of his dick. Her teeth edged around the tip, and then she sucked hard before the pressure of his hand moved her lower.

"Did I say I wanted to see you swallow me whole?" he asked gruffly, lust thickening in his throat. "I fucking should have."

She did just that.

Took him right to the damn base.

The way her tongue flattened against the underside of his shaft while her throat muscles worked to relax along his entire length was enough to drive him crazy.

Too late.

He already was.

Air rushed hard from Vera's nose as she watched him through the messy strands of her hair, and he kept her there with his hand. Mouth stretched wide around his cock. Water in her eyes.

He took the pressure off the back of her head at the same time he said, "Every fucking drop, Vera. Get it all out."

It'd been too long since Vaslav emptied his balls and if God was real and good, He knew she had the perfect mouth to do the job.

As soon as he let her take over without his physical direction, she proved him right. She used one hand to work the base of his shaft while she bobbed fast to meet her stroking fist. That wickedly sweet mouth of hers would only slow so she could tease the slit at the head of his dick, licking away precum and letting him see how she swept the beading drops along the tip of her tongue before they disappeared.

His approval came out in a long, guttural moan that he tried to bury into his hand and failed. He couldn't even look away from her anymore. The tightening in his spine and the familiar warmth pooling in his nuts said everything, anyway.

Vaslav had been more humiliated when he couldn't rid his erection earlier in the shower and she pretended not to notice than he was when he realized she was going to make him blow his load in a shamefully short amount of time.

Maybe it was her talent.

She *did* have a candy-sweet mouth, after all.

Really, it was just the fact that he hadn't been touched in years. Not like *this*. Not with a woman who hadn't been paid to do the job, frankly, or one that watched him with hungry eyes like Vera did.

"*Khristos*," he hissed, his neck falling back to the edge of the bucket chair.

Not even the sight of the ceiling could keep him from coming when he could feel the way her throat swallowed around him as she took him back to the base again.

"*Fuck*, don't you dare move," he uttered, his hand settling firmly to the back of her neck as all that tension came rushing out.

She took him beautifully.

Like a goddamn champ.

He only rolled his head a bit on the chair, just enough to watch her take the last drop before he let her go. She didn't even choke on his cum, or the force as which he'd released into the back of her throat, and she took her time sucking clean his shaft and tip before she released him with a soft *pop*. But the streaks down her cheeks from the tears that had escaped her eyes and her swollen lips did the most dangerous things to his self-control.

Then, she licked what remained of him away on her lips, too.

With a sinful little smile.

Vas let out a ragged exhale, yanking her into his lap before she could say a word otherwise. Her trembling lips found his while she settled in his lap, her legs straddling his waist. He could smell her now—how wet she was, the tangy scent of her wetness clung to the bit of air between them.

He stole one more kiss before biting lower, on her chin.

All she could do was sigh.

Sigh, and shift.

Thin cotton was no match for her slickness that had apparently pooled between her thighs while she'd sucked him off. Her panties were soaked through, and he could feel the fleshy outline of her pussy grinding along his still hard length. Every shift of her hips, seeking and finding that sweet spot, sent shivers racing over her shoulders and down her spine.

Pushing the wild hair out of her eyes, Vaslav asked her, "What do you want? Tell me."

"*Ebat'*."

The breathless word should have been music to his ears.

To fuck, she told him.

It just wasn't that simple.

"I'm not fucking you tonight."

And all at once, her movements stopped.

A pin could have dropped across the room, and he would have heard it. She couldn't hide the sting of rejection on her face, or maybe she just felt used as she started to pull back, one of her feet sliding to the floor.

"Then why would you—"

Vaslav couldn't let her do that. Not leave him or think the way she probably was. He snatched her by the wrist, pulling her into him and holding her around the waist as a fire came back to her eyes.

"Let me go," she demanded.

Quietly, sure, but firm all the same.

"Listen first," he said, the dopamine from his

orgasm wearing off and leaving him with the same pain it had kissed goodbye for a blissful minute. "*Listen*, yeah?"

Vera's trembling chin stiffened, but she still muttered, "I'm listening."

"Feel me, *kisska*." Her shuddering exhale when he rocked her body against his said she felt how hard he still was. All he needed to do was shift those sopping panties of hers to the side, and he'd fill her full. "I'm still hard after a half of a bottle of vodka, a Vicodin, and a load down your throat. I'd fuck you, and you'd feel me for a week, but I won't tonight. Not bare, Vera. I fuck no one bare."

"You don't have condoms."

Her head dropped, keeping her gaze from his as it settled in. To be honest, it was only a vague consideration in the back of his mind because he hadn't expected the night to turn out the way it had, let alone the overall trip.

That fight in her tense shoulders loosened only a little, and she whispered, "I'm on a shot, if that—"

"It doesn't matter."

He had rules for a reason.

That was one of them.

His fingers ticked under her chin, drawing her attention back to where he wanted it to be. *Only* on him. He bet his days would be far better if he could do this with her everyday; but men like him weren't afforded those sorts of pleasures without also paying a great price.

"*Hmm*, look at me, Vera."

"I am."

Yes, but was she seeing him?

Sometimes, those were two different things.

"This wasn't my intention—us doing this, I mean."

If that wasn't already clear.

He would have prepared better.

Her quiet somber mood melted into a whine of bliss when his one hand cupped her throat, and the other slipped under her panties and between her thighs to find that slick heat waiting for him. Greedy and hungry, she bucked into every touch, each stroke. She even bit her lip when he pinched a bit around the hood of her swollen clit, whispering shamelessly, "Do that again."

"You can't even pretend you didn't like to have a cock in your mouth, can you?" he asked as two of his fingers massaged into her clenching sex. If he was a lucky man, he would make sure Vera made a terrible mess of Pierre's bedroom chair. "No wonder you want to be a man's little slut—you just want to please. You want a third to really get you full, *kisska?*"

She was already rocking harder in his lap, taking what friction she could get from his hands and what he would give her with his fingers. "Yes, and don't hold back."

Oh, he wasn't the type for that.

"*Oh, my God ...* Vas, yes."

"Nobody," he told her, tracing her lips with his thumb again until she smiled, as shaky as it was, for him, "said you weren't going to get yours, too, kitten."

"That's my G-spot," she breathed when he found the fleshy spot on inside her cunt. "Y-you're gonna make me sq—"

"I know. This man's bedroom is going to smell like you for months." He added the third finger, she shuddered with a broken cry that was music to his

241

ears, and he massaged her inner wall harder as her hips started to shake. "Let's see just how wet you can get."

*

It had taken Vas entirely too long to find where Vera left his phone and jacket downstairs. He was less interested in the jacket than the phone, but since one was tucked inside the pocket of the other, he ended up back in the bedroom with both in his hands. Tossing the rumpled suit jacket over the corner of a dresser, he finally turned his attention back to the phone as he turned it on.

Instantly, he was drawn to the time on the screen. Crawling closer to half past three in the morning than he would like to admit, Vaslav was running out of time. The text he found waiting from Igor in his messages confirmed what he already knew.

Written in Russian, with few details, the message was simple, clear to the man it was meant for, and left him blowing out a hard exhale.

Confirmation sent through to the Italian. He'll be there at 5.

Vas looked at the time again.

He considered calling Igor; calling off the early-morning meeting was likely the right thing to do after the evening he'd had, and the fact his migraine still hadn't waned enough to give him any real relief.

The only thing that had done that was Vera.

And even she was busy, now.

His gaze skipped to the chair in the far corner of the bedroom, off to the left side of the bed. He could still picture her there—for a mind that was muddy and chaotic a lot of the time, his brain had done a damn good job of imprinting that woman into his memories. She was almost viscerally there, like he could still hear the way she'd almost squealed with her pleasure after he'd had her dripping a puddle down over his hands and onto the chair.

Oh, she'd soaked it.

The room *still* smelled like sex.

Sex they hadn't even had.

His cock had still been painfully hard then, too. Throbbing again and aching with that woman trembling in his lap. He almost reconsidered his rule about fucking raw, but even Vera couldn't break his very carefully crafted control in that regard.

Instead, he'd spun her around on his lap, pinned her back to his chest with an arm wrapped tight around her breasts, and rubbed another orgasm out of her while he grinded his cock into her tight ass like a teenaged boy getting his first dry hump from a girl.

Not that he was complaining.

He had come again like that. All up her back in hot spurts that painted her soft, porcelain skin with the dirtiness of his seed.

The only thing that worked to get his erection down *was* that second orgasm, and then a long walk through the dark floors of the apartment while he searched for his missing things. Not that it had been entirely effective—just the smell of Vera in that room was enough to get his dick twitching in the confines of the slacks that he'd pulled on before leaving the bedroom.

Good Christ.

She could kill him.

It'd be a hell of a way to die, though.

"How's the migraine?"

His distraction was going to be his downfall. The very fact he hadn't heard the shower turn off in the attached bathroom or heard Vera come to stand in the doorway connecting the two rooms told him that.

However, he barely gave it any thought because the sight of Vera naked with a towel in her hands and semi-dried hair falling in waves around her face was enough to remind him why he didn't care if he was distracted. He wasn't the type of man to get lost in a beautiful woman, but there was something different about this one.

Maybe it was that she *knew* she was beautiful. Or how her body looked in nothing but skin, with marks on her hips where he'd held a little too tightly as he came that last time.

Who knew what the reason was?

"Better," he lied. "It's a bit better."

She wrapped the towel around her body and took a step further into the room after she shut off the light to the bathroom. "Didn't you have business—wasn't that why you were coming to Paris?"

"Don't worry about that. Worry about getting some sleep. We're still flying out at ten tomorrow."

Or earlier.

It depended on how he felt.

Vera hesitated where she stood, not moving for the bed or even for the doorway to go to the room she'd been using during their stay. She gave him a second look, lingering on his bare feet and the slacks he'd left unzipped at his waist. "Aren't you coming to bed?"

"No, but you should."

Not that he would tell her, but she looked like she could use a few hours of sleep, or a lot more. The darkness under her eyes was prominent, and she'd stifled two yawns since she came out of the bathroom.

He bet she *was* exhausted.

After the night, and then him …

Well, who wouldn't be?

"Get some sleep," he told her, turning for the doorway. "That bed is open, if you don't want to walk down the hall."

"Would you stay if I wasn't in here?"

Vaslav was a lot of things—bluntly honest was just one of them. People often mistook that as him being cruel or mean because he was fine with pointing out how stupid he thought others were when they overlooked the obvious to feed their insecurities. Or rather, when he said it like he saw it.

Pausing in his step, he palmed his jaw as he rocked on the spot and considered whether he wanted to say something. She was lucky he even did that because no one else in his life was afforded that luxury.

"You do that a lot, no?" he asked.

Surprise brightened her face. "Do what?"

"*He won't fuck me or sleep with me*," Vaslav said, his mocking tone too high pitch for his own standards, but it was what it was. "You're a lot less interesting when you're swinging back and forth inside your irrational insecurities. The kind of men who like women that play those silly games wouldn't be standing here with an erection, Vera. *Again.* To a man like that, you'd have proved your worth the second your robe dropped to the ground."

She checked to see if he was lying, and he wasn't. He *still* would fuck her; still wanted to. And while he couldn't say whether he'd crawl in bed with her and fall asleep, he offered the only bed he'd been sleeping in, and he didn't have time to sleep.

Not that she was owed the knowledge of those things.

What more did she want?

Her mouth and jaws moved like she was chewing on words before she settled on saying, "That was mean."

"Or was it true?"

"They can be the same thing."

"Then maybe I don't care that it hurts when things are true," he returned flatly, "because I bet the next time I have to refuse you something, you won't look inside yourself for the reason why first. Not everything is about you."

Turning on his bare heels again to head for the door, he muttered under his breath, "You'd think a woman in your position wouldn't need to be spoon fed fucking self-respect and a backbone. Jesus Christ, you practically grew up on a stage."

He hadn't said it low enough because Vera's sharp gasp proved she'd heard the cruelty he so easily leveled upon her because she was naive. He couldn't pretend anything different; she barely knew him, had been sweet and kind even when he was not, had twenty years of living left to do to see the world through a perspective that *might* understand his, and none of that was her fault.

She'd not pursued him.

At the end of the day, Vera was there because he'd wanted her to be. She didn't understand that this was who he had no choice but to be. In pain, quick to snap with a mean insult just to end a conversation with a woman he hadn't even gotten to fuck because he didn't want her to blame herself for the way this had turned out.

Vas could feel—practically taste—how bitter his words were. Still, even seconds later, they remained heavy on his tongue. The second he'd said it … for the first time ever, he wished that he hadn't said it at all.

He didn't fault her for what she did next.

"*Po'shyol 'na hui—Fuck you.*"

Vera didn't yell the words, but it stung all the same. Her anger hissed like wind; the same way her slender figure did cutting past him before she left him behind in the bedroom without even a glare.

He'd have gone after her. Explained, even, that he'd lied about the state of his migraine, his stress was high, and he was sure that all of it would seem like excuses to her. The fact he was nasty, seemingly unapologetically so, was just a by-product of his awful method of coping.

Not all of it was good.

Instead of following her, he scratched at his beard and looked at the time on his phone; it had crawled beyond half past three.

Of course.

His gaze lifted to the doorway when a bedroom door slammed loudly down the hall.

Business first, he thought.

Everything else had to wait.

26.

Vera's eyes fluttered open to darkness, and the slam of a door. Having yanked open the window in the bedroom before she finally fell asleep on the four-poster bed with cloud-like white blankets and pillows, her naked body felt the nice chill from the breeze coming in, but it also brought something else.

A sound …

The low rumble of an engine.

She barely registered the time blinking on the digital clock beside the bed, the only light offered in the room. The red five-oh-five just didn't make sense to her overly exhausted brain as she pushed up from the bed to follow the sound coming in from the window.

She padded in bare feet across the cool hardwood floor to find that she had been right. It was the sound of a vehicle's engine that was carrying up to her spot—from a black two-door sedan that had parked in the side street along the fence that protected the apartment's backyard garden and paths from strangers.

Vera moved to close the window, but the shout of Italian made her pause. She couldn't understand or even see the two men talking in the alley below, so she pulled the window down to at least shut out the noise in the otherwise sleeping city.

Maybe she could get back to sleep.

If her bladder hadn't made itself known.

It took her way too long to find the rumpled t-shirt she'd used to sleep in the night before and since the bedroom at the end of the hall didn't have a private bathroom like the master, she was forced to open her door and head for the stairs. The only other bathroom was downstairs, full-size like the master, but she'd noticed it wasn't as lived in as the other.

The apartment was as quiet as it had been, and only dim pot lights along the ceiling helped her manage her way down the stairs. She was halfway down when she heard Vas.

"Mr. Messina, yes?"

"Call me Mario."

All at once, Vera stopped in the stairwell, every muscle in her body freezing. She sat on the ledge of a step as the two men with two distinct accents—one Russian, and one Italian—continued their conversation.

"You made me wait so long for a time and place that I was starting to think we were going to have a late brunch," the man Vaslav had called Mario said, his tone remaining cheerful.

"Too early for you, comrade?"

"Honestly?"

"I prefer it," Vaslav deadpanned.

"Not even God gets me out of bed before eight."

A dark, familiar chuckle echoed up the stairs. She knew it was Vaslav because the sound connected to her brain instantly and left her in a pile of shivers. Even her breath rattled. It was disconcerting how a man could be so mean, without even caring, and still manage to turn her on when they weren't even looking at one another face to face.

Who blessed him with that control?

"I'm not the kind of man who meets for brunch," Vaslav said then.

A throat cleared, and seconds ticked by.

"Not lunch or dinner, either?"

"Not particularly, but there's a fruit basket on the table. I'll even find you a knife, yes?"

"I do like to eat when I talk business," the unfamiliar man murmured. "Keeps the hands busy and on the table, you see?"

"I'll stand, you can eat, and we'll both see hands while we chat. Deal?"

"One might think your need to acquire my cocaine would mean you would bend over backward to ensure a good business partnership," Mario noted.

"Take my money, or don't," Vaslav uttered low. "That's what you fucking get from me. Very little else."

No wonder Vaslav hadn't been concerned about business earlier. Vera was acutely aware of the fact she shouldn't be sitting there eavesdropping on a conversation that was clearly meant to be private. It reminded her of being little and sneaking down the stairs of her childhood home to listen to the hissed conversations between the men who answered to her father.

The walls had ears.

"Your man is staying outside?" Vaslav asked.

"I *am* willing to play by your rules, Mr. Pashkov."

Again, silence took over the dimly lit apartment, growing stronger in heaviness by the time it reached Vera sitting on the step. She wondered if the Italian man had called Vaslav that and waited as long as he did to see if the Russian would offer him the same respect he had handed over earlier.

Nothing hard. Just his name. Like a friend might do.

Once more, the Italian cleared his throat.

Vaslav simply said, "The dining table, then?"

Even Vera could feel the tone of the meeting change between the two men. Unspoken, but thick and cold in the air.

There are no friends here.

*

A woman with any sense would have turned her ass around and took herself straight back to bed once she realized she was overhearing the private details of a long-term business transaction between two high-ranking criminals, but apparently Vera was not very smart after all. Because she never moved farther than the top of the stairwell. Even as her bladder continued to scream for relief, she curled herself into a ball, using the pressure of her arms around her stomach to hold in her pee so that she didn't have to move.

She knew she shouldn't hear.

She also shouldn't interrupt.

That could be worse.

Vera opted for the less dangerous option and ended up creeping to the top of the stairs where she sat in silence while the men talked in the dining are of the large kitchen. While she couldn't hear everything, she heard enough, and could piece together the rest without much trouble or effort.

Vas needed cocaine.

Mario produced and exported it. With a worldwide ring of smugglers at his fingertips ready to do his bidding. It was all very … *boring*. Shockingly so. From preparation, to packaging and packing, and how it would be hidden when it was smuggled into Russia as close to Moscow as possible. Someone even got a pencil and paper out to sketch some numbers. Right down to dimes and cents, because American currency was the only one the two men could settle on for a mutual method of payment.

All cash.

Millions delivered *monthly*.

Math made Vera want to gag.

She wasn't even being dramatic.

With her elbow resting on her knee, and her other arm still wrapped tight around her stomach to help keep her bladder under control, she almost fell asleep while her chin rested in her hand. It was only the sound of footsteps and laughter that had her blinking back awake faster than she could even comprehend.

God.

She needed some sleep.

Soon.

"One last thing," she heard Vaslav say downstairs.

"What's that?" Mario replied.

"Was it just for the bragging rights—to say that you'd done it?"

"I beg your pardon?"

A harsh sigh followed before Vaslav said, "That you could do this; pull me away from Russia and sit down with the beast."

"You aren't the only man who needs to flex his control."

"But I am the only man who can get your cocaine into my country," Vaslav returned. "And according to my information, you need that. A new boss, too young, no wife—"

"That's quite enough," Mario said, quiet but still firm.

Vaslav hummed under his breath. "You need to show you can grow; prove your place before someone deems you unworthy. I may be just one aspect, but it only takes one wall to crumble an already weak house. You see, a few years ago *I* was the new boss with the bloodstained seat, and vengeful men waiting to kiss my fucking feet. It would be wise to remember that."

Tension silenced the two again.

But not for long.

"Fair enough," Mario muttered first. "The Frenchman will be happy to know he's made another successful deal. I heard he likes the cut you give him off the top."

Vaslav's dry chuckles ended in a low grunt. "Look around—Pierre already knew he was going to get paid."

A second passed.

Then, two.

"This is his place?"

"It appears so," Vaslav replied. "Have a safe flight."

"Hmm, and you also, Mr. Pashkov."

Vera stayed at the top of the stairs long after the two men ended their meeting, and the front door had clicked shut. After Vaslav headed back into the kitchen and turned a tap on, she was suddenly reminded of the issue she didn't even know how she managed to forget.

Her full bladder.

Positive she would have time to slip down the stairs and to the bathroom at the rear of the apartment without being noticed, she did just that. But her feet barely hit the bottom level before the loud heaving in the kitchen sent her running that way.

She found Vaslav vomiting violently into the stainless-steel trash can while the half-filled glass of water sat nearby on the corner of the kitchen island. He couldn't possibly have heard her coming; his heaving was so loud, it could wake neighbors.

"Vas, are you okay?"

She touched his back at the same time he leaned further into the can to spill what remained of the water into the black bag. He spat and swore.

Every *fuck* became louder than the last, and he didn't shove her away, but it was like he didn't see her at all when his fist slammed down into the marble countertop, either. His anger should have scared her, but she was more concerned with the clear vomit he wiped away from his mouth and the freshly bruised knuckles he drove into the side of his head with enough force to make her wince.

"*Stop*," she told him when he hit himself again. "*Vas, stop it!*"

"Fucking *fuck*," he snarled again, massaging his knuckles way too hard into his temple even as she tried to pull his arm away. "I gotta ... I need to br—"

His words cut off with another heave that sent him spinning toward the trash can again, but on the way, he knocked over the glass of water, sending it spilling across the countertop, soaking the other items she hadn't even noticed there.

"The passports," Vera cried, reaching to pull them out of harm's way before they were destroyed as Vaslav vomited into the garbage again. "Why are these here?"

She didn't get an answer, but she tried to help him again anyway.

Had he been in pain the whole time the Italian was there? He'd hid it well, if so, because she couldn't even hear it in his voice. Did that mean he'd lied to her earlier when he told her his migraine was better?

"What can I do?" she asked him. "Just tell me how to help."

Because she still would; even though he had been mean and cruel, and didn't even apologize, she still wanted to help this man.

He clearly needed it.

He needed someone.

Vaslav still didn't act like he heard her, and her feeble attempts to help did nothing to pull his fist away from his head. She fell to the floor with him when he crumpled into a heap against the kitchen island, her arms wrapped around one of his as she tucked into his side when he started to groan.

And that sound?

It hurt her deep.

Like she could feel the way he hurt, too. Agony he couldn't escape.

"I'm not going anywhere," she told him even as her kidneys screamed in pain. "I'll do anything you need me to, okay?"

If it would help …

"Call Igor," was all he managed to say.

Spit through clenched teeth, barely even audible, and every word was a struggle.

Call Igor.

The pain had to be bad.

After all, he wasn't dead.

*

"Wake up, sleepy head."

Vera blinked awake in just enough time to feel a soft kiss press down on the crown of her head. By the time she'd gained her bearings enough to realize someone had covered her with a white blanket, and the view rushing outside the porthole window said they had touched down in Moscow, Vaslav was already back in his seat.

Like he hadn't woken her up at all.

Stretching her arms and yawning out what remained of her sleepy confusion, she met the gaze of the man in the white leather seat across from hers.

"A nap helped me, too," he told her.

Vera tried to smile, but it was small and weak.

He didn't miss it.

"I'm sorry."

Vera didn't move an inch, not even when the flight attendant strolled down the aisle of the rocking jet. "For what?"

"You make it harder when I have to explain."

"Apologies are useless if you don't know what you're apologizing for."

Vaslav scrubbed a hand over his mouth as he

watched the scene outside the now-taxiing jet. "Your passport, for starters."

Her heart dropped.

But then his gaze swung back to her, and he added, "I know I was unnecessarily mean to you, but what good is saying sorry if it's going to happen again, Vera?"

"You could try not to."

Vaslav laughed a dark sound, shaking his head. "You don't have any idea …"

"You could fill me in?"

Sometimes having a conversation with this man felt like the blind leading the blind; she had no idea where he was going, or if he even knew.

"You mean, prove how awful I really am, yeah?" he asked.

Vera's brow furrowed as she bundled the soft blanket into a ball in her lap. "I don't understand."

"Of course you don't," the man muttered. "You were collateral. Depending on how the Italian reacted—or what he tried to bring into the meeting to test how far he could push me—I had you."

She blinked. "What?"

Not once had he mentioned the fact he believed she'd overheard his meeting. In fact, after the early-morning call to Igor, she focused on packing and arranging their things while Vaslav hid under a blanket, in total darkness with as much silence in the apartment as was possible, until they had no choice but to leave because the car arrived. She didn't even message Hannah for breakfast like she'd promised to.

Something else she would have to explain.

Surely.

"What, did you think I'm stupid?" Vas asked her.

"I never said th—"

"You had to be listening. How else would you be so fast to get to the kitchen, hmm? How long?"

Vera refused to drop his hard stare. "I was trying to pee."

For a second, she thought he *might* crack a smile.

Instead, he stuck the proverbial knife deeper than ever into her heart. "Your father controls major international ports in New York that Mario Messina uses to get a great deal of his product into the United States. Whatever their personal connection or private business dealings are to make that possible, well, I didn't give a damn. But you see, I had you—a good enough connection to your father that just the knowledge I could use you as leverage would be enough to ensure the Italian didn't cross the line … Frankly, I didn't need much else. Not that the meeting swung that way in the end, after all. I didn't need to leverage you."

"Collateral," she echoed.

He grunted under his breath and looked upward when the seatbelt light blinked on again for no apparent reason as the state of the plane hadn't really changed. "Useful was the word I used to you, actually."

Disbelief swept through her.

How could she forget?

"*Useful,*" she parroted.

Not kindly, though.

"And just how would you have used me as collateral to that man?" Vera decided to ask.

Vaslav didn't even think about it. "It wouldn't matter. A threat to deliver you in pieces would have done the job."

Her heart squeezed painfully.

"Whether it was a threat I would follow through on is another matter," he said more to himself than her. Vera still heard it perfectly fine.

"You only wanted me to come along because I was useful?"

Why?

Because she was the daughter of a dangerous, important man? A connection he could manipulate for his own selfish gain. As coldly, cruelly, and uncaringly as he had insulted her after being so intimate with her, this felt just the same.

She was just a pawn.

A piece to move in a game she hadn't even asked to play. How was that fair?

"It can be both," he returned as the jet shuddered a bit before it slowed yet again. All she wanted to do was get off at that moment. Instead, she was stuck staring at the man across from her, sharing his air and space, and wondering if he really was just a goddamn monster. "I can want you, and you can be useful, too."

Hadn't he said the same thing the night before? Something can be mean—even hurt—and still be true?

"It can be both," Vaslav repeated even as Vera stayed silent. "And I hope you know that it is."

She didn't know anything about him at all. That was the stark reality staring her in the face.

He stared her in the face, and even though she couldn't look away, although she knew in her heart that she should, Vera didn't.

He might very well be a monster, but she'd held him in her hands when he was entirely human, too.

"I need a wife," he said without warning. "A companion, more than anything. A legal barrier between me, the doctors, what's left of my family … the *mafiya*, too. I need the protection a legal marriage will give me in the coming months as I begin to work on cleaning up a few of my affairs." Then, he shrugged, lifting one eyebrow high when he added, "Or years, we'll see how it goes."

We'll see how it goes?

"See how what goes?"

Vaslav drummed his fingers to the jet's plush seat. "Life—or rather, what remains of mine."

What?

"Are you insane?" she asked.

"Diagnosed as such once, yes."

He offered the news with no emotional inflection.

"Like I said, I am in need of a wife."

"And how does that have anything to do with me?"

"I need a wife," Vaslav reiterated for the umpteenth time, meeting her gaze, "and I think you will do."

The entire scene was surreal. He couldn't be serious. Where had that idea even come from?

Her reply rushed out in a nervous laugh. "I'm not going to marry you."

Not for a few months.

And certainly not for *years*.

Vaslav smiled, his head tipping to the side so he could peer out the porthole where Moscow waited to welcome them home. "Oh, *kisska* … but won't you?"

27.

"Do you know why I liked you?"

The near-constant stream of chatter from the driver's seat came to a halt the second Vaslav posed the question. The thing was, he really wanted an answer.

Because he couldn't remember.

"No," Igor eventually said.

Too quietly, maybe.

Even Igor's massive shoulders tensed enough that his boss could see from his position in the backseat of the familiar SUV. If it were another man, Vas might have let the whispers of paranoia become louder to his mind about what his man's actions meant, but it was Igor.

Of all people, Vaslav trusted him.

At the very least, to always do the right thing.

"Hmm," he muttered in the backseat, turning his attention to the window and the passing scenery. Out of the corner of his eye, he could see how Igor's gaze shifted to the rearview mirror, but he opted not to continue the conversation further.

A smart choice, really.

"Can I take your random question to mean you weren't listening to me?" Igor asked. "Would you like me to repeat—"

"Do I ever want you to repeat things, Igor?"

Silence answered the rhetorical question. Not for long, of course, but the brief period of reprieve at least allowed Vaslav to survey the newspaper that had been folded and left in the seat beside his. Front page up, with a name sticking out amongst the sea of black letters on a white background.

Nico.

He suspected if he picked it up and turned the newspaper over that he would find his old friend's death had finally been properly announced to the city of Moscow—and the rest of the country—along with the fact he'd been murdered. Why else would they put the well-respected lawyer's picture and name on the front page, if not to connect it to a previous story about a body being found in the canal?

I gave you that, anyhow, he thought, wondering if his dead friend could even hear him wherever his soul was now. *Another front-page story, Nico.*

"Good to see they finally got around to identifying the body."

"I expect the funeral details to be forthcoming," Igor muttered as he blew through a four-way with little signage or lights to control the different directions of traffic. A dangerous thing to do on the streets of Russia.

Neither man even blinked.

"Soon?"

Igor nodded in the front. "Within a couple of days, yeah."

Good.

Funerals were the one social event that Vaslav still liked to attend. If only because it always made a point to anyone who needed one made to them about just what he could do. After all, the only funerals he attended were of those that he'd killed.

In one way or another ...

"Mira's already called ahead to your tailor in the city about something new for the occasion," Igor said when Vaslav didn't continue their chat.

He didn't reply to *that*, either.

It would require unnecessary effort that he didn't care to expend. The handful of people who had the unfortunate responsibility of having their life tied to Vaslav for however long his would last didn't need him to validate what they already knew. Whether it was what they should be doing, or what they needed to be doing at any given moment—didn't matter.

Vaslav should have been comforted by the sight of a familiar landscape beyond the blacked-out windows of the SUV. To be home, in his motherland, was to be the *safest*. As much as was possible, anyway. He used to travel out of Russia often, even with the scattered, frequent migraines, but the last handful of years had made that more difficult.

And then there was the newest thing, too.

The seizures.

The very last thing he needed when he *was* able to get out of Russia undetected for business was unexpected medical problems.

"This is going to be another fucking Abram situation all over again," Igor said, dragging Vaslav out of his thoughts in the worst possible way.

"What did you just say?"

"Hear me out."

The rushed way Igor tried to appease Vaslav said he knew exactly where he had fucked up, but it was already too late.

"Pull over," Vaslav demanded.

Everybody had a line; he just happened to have several. That was one of them.

"What, Vas, we almost out of the county limit—"

"Pull over right now or I will use the headrest of your seat to beat the back of your skull open so that the next thing I say, your entire brain will be able to hear it."

That did it.

Vas used the handle on the door to steady himself when Igor yanked the vehicle onto the side of the road with little warning. Two cars raced past the SUV, rocking the vehicle from the speed, and he shoved the rear door open the first moment he could. Had he cared even one bit about the fact his migraine had been gone when he opened his eyes after a nap on the jet, then he would have stayed inside the vehicle.

A bright sun blinded him from overhead, deepening his already-raging scowl but never deviating him from his task. Igor took too goddamn long to also get out of the vehicle, so Vaslav ripped him out after the man cracked his door.

"Jesus Christ, relax!" Igor shouted when Vaslav shoved him along the front of the SUV. In his effort to catch himself from falling to the cracked asphalt, Igor stumbled against the hood, knocking loose the gun that must have been tucked into his waistband.

Paris had taken another thing from him.

A decent weapon.

Snatching the Glock up from the ground, he wasn't shocked to find the safety off, and a fully loaded magazine inserted. He didn't need to rack it when he pointed the gun at Igor's face as the man straightened up with his palms out. Igor didn't take him seriously, however, until his finger wrapped around the trigger.

"Ah, fucking hell … Vas, come on," the man muttered.

"*What* did you say?" Vaslav asked as the two rounded the front of the SUV. Igor came to a stop with his back facing the hood.

"This is going to be another Abram situation if you don't chill the fuck out," Igor said calmly.

It was too public.

"If only that mattered."

Igor sucked in a short gulp of air, and his gaze darted away from Vaslav long enough for him to know the man believed he was going to die. Another car rushed past, and he didn't didn't need to look over his shoulder to check for brake lights, either.

"I just …" Igor squeezed his eyes shut, coughing out a laugh when the barrel of the gun touched his forehead. "You didn't listen to me then, either, Vas. Maybe you don't remember that, too, huh?"

He hated Igor for that; for being right every time. Especially when Vaslav wasn't listening.

"It's *not* going to be another Abram situation," Vaslav said, shoving the gun hard into Igor's chest, dropping it where the man caught it with a breath of relief.

"You're sure fucking acting like it."

Igor had called that at his back while Vaslav headed for the rear door he'd left open, but he heard it all the same. He let the rock of the SUV be his reply when he slammed the door shut after stepping inside.

The two didn't speak again until Igor was back on the road, and they'd left the scene far behind them.

"You're erratic," Igor said from the front. "You do things and tell me later. If you tell me at all. I know you're not taking your meds right, and you won't go to the doctors. How's the paranoia, boss?"

Vaslav's gaze narrowed on the sliver of his reflection in the blacked-out glass. "Fuck off," he warned.

The only one he'd give.

Igor shook his head, and the SUV's engine roared as the speed increased.

"Nico had to go," Vaslav said after a moment. "He disobeyed me; fed the hand of my enemy. He didn't give me another choice."

"If you hadn't left Feliks alive for as long as you have, then we wouldn't be in this situation in the first damn place."

"He deserved to suffer, too."

And he did.

For years, Feliks had been a pariah in a world that had once adored him. Now he was the disgraced son of a dead man barely able to make a living while he *wished* he was dead. And all because Vaslav had said so—because he said any Abramov was an untouchable. Like sewage mud, anyone who got too close would stink.

And Vas would know.

Like Nico.

Except Nico was not like the time Vaslav had killed his father-in-law and practically nailed a death notice to Feliks' infamous Swan House doors.

"I killed him publicly, delivered his head to his son on a weekday, and had a doctor's office bombed across the city all in the same day," Vaslav intoned flatly from the back seat. "I practically handed them the evidence."

"And an insanity plea," his friend uttered.

Vas ignored that.

"This won't be the same."

"The second you walk into that funeral; it *will* be the same. They'll know. And if not the officials dragging you into court again, it'll be the brotherhood. Whoever's been watching ... waiting," Igor added quieter at the end. "You start dropping bodies all over Moscow, and it's gonna happen again, Vas. It'll be prison or the mad house. One way or the other."

Igor was so good at saying things without actually *saying* them. He might as well have screamed *now you can't kill Feliks; there's already one too many dead.*

"*Enough*, Igor."

Igor's exhale rattled.

Even he heard the nerves.

"It won't be the same," Vaslav said once he felt the anger that had been steadily building in his chest start to ebb.

"Please tell me how?"

"This time, my wife won't be dead."

He swore he heard the crack of Igor's neck when the man's head jerked up. He didn't bother to check to see if Igor was watching him again in the rearview mirror, and instead, just assumed he was.

"What?"

The confusion made him chuckle.

"Vas, Irina is d—"

"I know she's dead. I said my wife. I didn't specify which wife, did I?"

He did look to the rearview, then, and sure enough, Igor's stony gaze waited for him.

"The only thing that would have been different if Irina had been alive was your estate, Vas. Legally, she could have protected that a bit more but, I mean—"

"Yes, she could have protected me. From doctors, lawyers, and everyone else that was being paid by my fucking mother from a bank account she didn't even know existed before that day. *Remember*?"

It was a bit dirtier than that.

More traumatic, too.

But it wouldn't happen again.

"Except she said no," Vaslav added, sinking further into the seat.

"Who—*what*? What in the hell happened in Paris?"

"Vera. I need a wife, and she said no."

It took Igor fifteen entire seconds to reply. Vaslav counted. "Did you ask?"

He considered that.

"Define *ask*."

"Jesus Christ. You really are fucking crazy. How did you even come up with that?"

"No, not really. I only need to show her why she's wrong."

"Vas—"

"I assume it'll be easy," he continued.

Depending on the way he went about it. Although, she could still make it hard.

Everybody had their prerogative.

"Well, when they're dragging your ass through the streets, at least she'll be something beautiful beside you to look at," Igor said under his breath.

Vas laughed. "Like beauty and the beast. How does the next part go? I'm supposed to steal her and lock her away?"

"Nobody said anything about—"

"Oh, don't worry. That woman will come willingly."

Even if he had to make her.

*

Loving Vaslav and Vera's story? Part Two coming soon …

Xo,
BK

ABOUT THE AUTHOR

The author of too many novels to count, Bethany-Kris is a Canadian, lover of much, and mother to four sons, a glaring of cats, and a pack of dogs. A small town in Eastern Canada where she was born and raised is where she has always called home. With her boys under her feet, a snuggling cat, barking dogs, and a spouse calling over his shoulder, she is nearly always writing something ... when she can find the time.

Find where to follow BK and keep up to date with all her book news at www.bethanykris.com.

OTHER BOOKS

The Beast of Moscow Saga

The Beast of Moscow

The Darkest Lies Trilogy

The Agreement
The Promise
The Marriage

After Another Trilogy

One Step After Another
One Breath After Another
One Second After Another

Boykov Bratva

Fractured Ties
Essence of Fear

The Guzzi Legacy

Corrado
Alessio
Chris
Beni
Bene
Marcus
The Firsts: A Guzzi Legacy Companion Novel
The Guzzi Legacy: Vol 1
The Guzzi Legacy: Vol 2

Renzo + Lucia

Privilege
Harbor
Contempt
Forever
Cusp
Renzo + Lucia: The Complete Trilogy

Andino + Haven

Duty
Vow
One Last Time
Andino + Haven: The Complete Duet

John + Siena

Loyalty
Disgrace
John + Siena: The Complete Duet
John + Siena: Extended

Cross + Catherine

Always
Revere
Unruly
The Companion
Naz & Roz

Guzzi Duet

Unraveled, Book One
Entangled, Book Two
Cara & Gian: The Complete Duet

DeLuca Duet

Waste of Worth: Part One
Worth of Waste: Part Two

Standalone Titles

Pink
Pretty Lies
Dirty Pool
Effortless
Inflict
Cozen
Captivated
Dishonored

Donati Bloodlines

Thin Lies
Thin Lines
Thin Lives
Behind the Bloodlines
The Complete Trilogy

Filthy Marcellos

Antony
Lucian
Giovanni
Dante
Legacy
A Very Marcello Christmas
The Complete Collection

Seasons of Betrayal

Where the Sun Hides
Where the Snow Falls
Where the Wind Whispers
Seasons: The Complete Seasons of Betrayal Series

Gun Moll Trilogy

Gun Moll
Gangster Moll
Madame Moll

The Chicago War

Deathless & Divided
Reckless & Ruined
Scarless & Sacred
Breathless & Bloodstained
The Complete Series
Maldives & Mistletoe

The Russian Guns

The Arrangement
The Life
The Score
Demyan & Ana
Shattered
The Jersey Vignettes

FANTASY ROMANCE

The Hunted: A 9INE REALMS Novel

Find more on Bethany-Kris's website at
www.bethanykris.com.